Screams Before Dawn

Heinrich von Wolfcastle

For my nighttime writing Buddy

CONTENTS

A Scream Before Dawn   3

What Happened   15

Bird's the Word   40

She Said Her Name Was Spookie   60

Vultures of the Aftermath   70

The White Cross on Resurrection Drive   74

Of God, Monsters, and Men   78

Employee Assistance Program   92

Things in the Attic   101

Marvin's Tavern   125

The Last Day on Earth   146

Ambassadors of Ambrosia   164

ACKNOWLEDGMENTS

This collection was written with gratitude to those who provided their creative and editorial talents as well as their overall support. Specifically, I want to thank Rob Berger, Jessica Bloom, RWB, Gail Chandler, and Tim Duggan.

A SCREAM BEFORE DAWN

The rabid stench of decay seeped itself into every thread of every tapestry to be found in the room. It permeated cloth, carpet, and wallpaper; there was no escaping it. The odor was so horribly thick and bitter that anyone not yet used to the smell was left to feel as if the inside of their mouth was sweating.

Mildred had been confined to her bedroom, immobile, for several weeks. She was alone and positioned in her bed to look out the window. She had no television, but watching the children play their games in the spring weather kept her mind from roaming too far. On her last day, a Sunday, the neighborhood boys and girls were all chasing each other about their yards.

A woman can go to church her whole life on a Sunday and never once consider that it could be her death day. And how many times did we walk through a calendar year never knowing which day would be her final one? The day matters, you see, because on most days, a nurse would be there with her. They came five days a week. But, Sunday was not a scheduled day; that was the nurses' church day. It was of no worry to Mildred though, as she had been feeling stronger as of late. In fact, she was thinking about canceling her nursing care altogether.

3

Towards the end, all Mildred really wished for was to be able to open the window and feel some fresh air – to feel anything other than the settling of dust on her and her orange and yellow bed sheets. She couldn't really express this wish in words, but I knew. She did not ask for much. She was ill, after all.

Every now and again a friend or neighbor stopped by to sit in that large orange chair next to the bed and chat about nothing of particular relevance. Mildred was unable to respond. But, it didn't really matter what was said anyway; the important thing was that someone was there with her, wasn't it? Mildred felt that. I felt that.

That window was all that Mildred had to keep her busy. It may as well have been a television anyway, given the way the dust hovered in the air like the static from a poorly tuned station filling her room. A shame that such a beautiful creature should meet its demise in such an unceremonious place.

The children she watched thought nothing of her. They could see her through the window but never really looked twice at the tube that penetrated her neck. They never stared and never minded.

Every so often, Mildred would start to drift into a sleep, but it was never a restful sleep for her, more like a tease of what restful sleep would be like. When she would start to nap, I would close my eyes too – feeling the way the dust danced about the room. I suppose I would also drift off a bit, following thoughts about the way things used to be.

Mother was never told to expect a girl, and she was bewildered in her effort to raise two by herself, especially when she had anticipated only one. And *father* was a label no man earned from us beyond biology. Perhaps it was for this reason, and in combination with the shame of having a child out of wedlock, that few people knew of Mildred or me. Childhood certainly had its challenges for the two of us, including repeated meetings with Mother's paddle. For these reasons, and others, we confided in one another and no one else.

We played well together, and our dolls lived full lives under our care. When we outgrew our dolls, we took to writing – creating plays and elaborate narratives for our play things. Mother disapproved, but we persisted in spite of her. Eventually, we reached local fame not for our narratives, but for our ability with improvisation. The true secret, the *true* secret, is that we knew one another's thoughts.

Mildred would sit on our stoop and wait for a wealthy-looking man or woman to walk by. She would call out, "No secrets are safe! For a coin, I can tell you your phone number by just knowing your name!" A precocious little girl like her earned the attention of many passersby. They would approach with a scoff on their face. But, once she heard their name, it was as if *I* heard their name too. Only, I was tucked away back in our bedroom with the telephone directory. And, when I *knew* a phone number, Mildred *knew* it too.

Wondering how we afforded our dolls, Mother would inspect our purses and find them filled with coin. When she learned the secrets of our trade, she brought her paddle to our behinds and cursed at us, "She who sups with the devil should have a long spoon." *Whack!*

As we grew older, potential lovers would talk to us of *soul mates*, but the discussion was futile. Mildred had me, and I had her. We had already found our "other halves," you see? Alas, what was to be our life together was taken from us.

Mother's body was found some months after her life had ended. I had gone to the market to purchase fabric for costumes for a new play we were creating. Meanwhile, Mildred was in our bedroom reviewing our writing when Mother, drunk from wine at the local church, thought to take the paddle to her for the second time on the day – perhaps mistaking her for me. In a fit of defiance, Mildred moved from Mother's swing and grabbed the paddle from her hand. "You slag, you fucking dog!" Mother screamed at her.

"A slag, am I, Mother?" Mildred returned.

"A slag, a wench. A shame I brought you to this world, isn't it?" Mother yelled, reaching for the paddle.

Without a retort, Mildred brought the paddle down on Mother's head, announcing a thud and cracking her skull. What was once a tool for punishment became lethal when turned on its side to strike with its dense edge. Mother's body fell to the ground in a pool of its own fluids, which was where it remained until the bobbies came in response to a call regarding the smell of decomposition coming from our flat.

Yes, I was away when Mildred brought the paddle down upon Mother. But, the same way that Mildred and I *know* one another's thoughts is the same way *we* brought the paddle down over her head. We brought it down *again*, and *again*, and *again*.

When the bobbies came, I was home and Mildred was at the market. As such, Mildred lived a full life – free to travel and create! I could not have been more excited for her, as her life and her work were my life and my work too, you see? I saw life through her eyes, while my own eyes stared blankly at institution walls. Mildred had a mad creative rage, an art that demanded expression. On occasion, as her eyes, I had the privilege of watching her create her art, building on the portfolio that started with Mother. It was a sight to see and a rhythm to dance to.

Sometimes, Mildred would invite me to share the paddle as she brought it down on the heads of gentlemen callers, but I was not a musician the way that she was. I would hesitate in the swing, which altered the timing of it all. For me, the pleasure was in the sound she made with it. I suppose the *thudding* was like an anniversary song that honoured mother's passing. For each time it played, it never lost its appeal or that hypnotic grip that commanded me to move to its rhythm. In her later years with her health difficulties, it was a song I longed to hear while Mildred remained bedridden.

On her final Sunday, Mildred awoke from a light afternoon nap, and through steel bars and concrete – across miles of ocean – I awoke with her. It was the sound of breaking glass and a doorknob rattling from the kitchen that spurred our attention. I sat in my hospital bed, listening through Mildred's ears. Footsteps. Heavy shoes – two sets of them – paced up and down the hall of Mildred's home. A kitchen cabinet door swung open and slammed shut. A bathroom door opened and crashed into the wall. Bathroom cabinets and drawers were emptied.

"Where the fuck is it, man?" one voice called out. He sounded like a teenage boy.

"I don't know, maybe in her room," another voice answered. He also sounded like a teenage boy.

"You're sure this bitch is comatose, right?" the first voice asked.

"Yeah man. She might even be dead. Just lays here all day," the second one answered. "Just trust me, there's a couple of nurses that come by during the week, but that's it," he assured. Their shoes made their way towards Mildred's bedroom.

"What kinda shit do you think they have her on?" the first one asked.

"Oxy, at least," the second voice answered. The door to Mildred's bedroom was open. Footsteps approached on the carpet of her room.

"God, smells like death in here," the first one said. He walked across the room and stood at the foot of Mildred's bed and paused to glance at her. He looked to be about six feet tall, gangly in his growing body. He had blonde hair that crept out from under a red hat with white lettering. The sun reflected off the gold-plated chain laying over his black shirt, which strained Mildred's eyes. "You awake, lady?" he asked.

Mildred said nothing.

"Dude, don't talk to her," the second one said. This second one was shorter, and had spiked black hair. A tattoo of something ran down the back right side of his neck.

"Where's your pills, old lady?" Red Hat asked.

Mildred said nothing.

"Don't talk to her," Neck Tattoo said with annoyance in his tone. He punched his friend in the arm on his way towards Mildred's bathroom.

"She's looking at me," Red Hat said. He leaned forward and squinted at Mildred.

"Dude, shut up. I got 'em. Let's get out of here," Neck Tattoo called back.

"Man, I don't think she's in a comber. She's looking at me," Red Hat repeated.

"Let's just get the hell out," Neck Tattoo said. His footsteps echoed as he made his way down the hall.

"Man, she can ID us," Red Hat said under his breath, more to himself than to his friend who had already left.

Mildred said nothing.

Red Hat leaned in close and squinted at her again, and then he scanned the room to assess the equipment around him. There was sweat on his upper lip. He looked out the window where kids were playing and then back at Mildred. He leaned in one last time, put his hand to her throat, pulled something from her, and then ran from the room and out of the house.

Mildred's ventilator sounded an alarm. And, without warning, she began to suffocate. The ventilator appeared to still be working, but it was undeniably getting harder for Mildred to breathe. In fact, the more she focused on her breathing, the more difficult it became. Red Hat had pulled the hose loose from her ventilator to her tracheostomy, and with every passing second of panic, her situation was becoming that much more critical.

I raised Mildred's arm to reach for something – anything. In a panic-induced daze, I brought her hands to

8

her throat as if I were trying to remove some invisible assailant's grip on her, but there was nothing to be removed. Her eyes rolled frantically around the room, dizzying me, as her lungs failed to inflate. Her coughs bounced off the flower-patterned walls.

A sharp high-pitched whistle cut through the still room as Mildred quickened her breath. The dust that surrounded her stopped and froze in position. Outside, the girls jumping rope slowed to a halt, leaving the jumper hovering in mid-air. While gasping for oxygen, Mildred reached back and pushed off of her bed in an attempt to sit up. Her mouth opened and closed as if mouthing the words to some final plea. When she finally sat up, she found herself only wishing to lie back down as she continued her struggle to breathe.

Mildred's gaze settled on the windows outside where children played their games and drew with chalk on the sidewalk. They laughed amongst themselves as mothers brought out lemonade and homemade cupcakes. Their shrieks of joy and shrill laughter seemed to rattle the windows of Mildred's room.

The sun poured through the window, highlighting the hanging dust particles. And, in this moment of adrenaline, Mildred's hands and legs began to fade away. A feeling of lightness took them over. Everything felt warm. It was a new feeling and a surprisingly welcome one.

And that was the trickiest part of it all. She was fighting for her dear life; I was fighting for her life. But the numbness was so calming. She blinked her eyes faster and opened them wider – still fighting. But at the same time, her vision grew darker.

Without notice, the lock on the world broke, sending time into a fury to catch up with itself. The dust in the air whirled about, and the children's laughter resumed with greater intensity as the whipping of the jump rope cracked against the cement over and over with growing haste. The noise was unbearable.

Mildred's view of the room fell off balance. Spots filled her vision, and her sight continued to dim. The growing darkness seemed to take her over, but it was a calming dark, and the hesitant numbness persisted.

Mothers continued to smile at their children as Mildred barely held on to her life. Her eyes opened wide as she waved her arms about. If she could borrow just one breath from those kids, she thought, just one of their laughs that seemed to roll out of their mouths with such ease, then she might be all right. But, alas, she fell back into her pillows and allowed the growing calm to consume her.

2

It was then, in the wake of her dying breath, that I was alone for the first time. They released me some weeks later. Fitting, somehow, that I would finally return to the world to take Mildred's place after I was locked away for so long for Mother's murder. But do not let the irony fool you; there is no greater peace being held hostage in a mental institution instead of prison. The horrors I – and the other residents – experienced there were greater than any deed that brought us there.

The violence we endured will echo those halls for all eternity. Patients deemed too unsafe for the doctors to work with had their hands and feet bound and then secured to adult-sized cribs. If not bound to a crib, then they would lock us away in an isolation chamber for hours or days at a time where we would shit ourselves without access to a toilet. But, somehow, that was safest.

You did not want a doctor's attention, you see. Because if you had their attention, then you might get injected with some drug that puts you to sleep and leaves you feeling like your body is going to fall out of its skin. If they wanted you awake, then they would hold you down and strap you to a table to electrocute you. You would know who recently had their brain zapped by their broken bones. The seizures from the electricity caused limbs to fracture in their flailing. Then there was the lobotomy. There was no coming back from that one. Those who were lobotomized became shuffling, drooling, zombies.

Perhaps the worst form of the doctors' attention was their taking advantage of us sexually. The acts they inflicted upon us were terrible. Whether forced or manipulated did not matter; it was all horrific. Even worse than enduring the deeds performed were the moments afterwards, when your body feels foreign and shameful to you, as if it betrayed you by somehow bringing about what happened. Many times afterwards, I disappeared into Mildred for comfort while she dressed me and soothed me, bringing my arms over my chest in a hug. I knew it was her in my arms, embracing me.

That kind of abuse stopped when Mildred took it upon herself to resolve the issue with one doctor in particular. You might ask how Mildred could use my body to make her music in the hospital without her paddle, but her art came naturally to her. Her work with the doctor was an answer to a question I once posed to her, "What if a song were made to be a painting instead?" The piece was so compelling in its use of color and abstraction that no one in the hospital dared to accuse any patient for the murder. Mildred always seemed to have a way with escaping any of the blame that might follow her deeds, and I consider myself fortunate that her grace extended to me, in addition to her tenderness and care. Had I not had my connection to Mildred – our bond – I suppose I would have hanged myself as so many others had. Even in my newfound independence, thoughts of death followed me, for what was I without my sister? Alas, first there was business to attend to.

My first act of freedom was to move my belongings to Mildred's home in the States and to reside there myself. The camaraderie we shared all of our lives was not absent in her death, and I thought I might find her there. But, what I found instead was that the house was to be reclaimed by the bank and was in a condition of deterioration. The glass that had broken and fallen to the ground at the side door was tracked throughout the home in trails of repeated footprints. The flickering hallway light revealed garbage and beer cans and cigarette butts burnt into the carpet. Mildred's bedroom had the curtains closed, and it was empty except for an uncovered mattress in the corner of the room. A dirty syringe and spoon resided upon it.

If there were any blessing resultant of my institutionalized years, it was in the gained practice of waiting. In Mildred's room, I stood and waited for minutes. For hours. For days.

3

The side door swung open, and glass crunched under the pressing of stepping shoes. A plastic bag of goods was placed on the kitchen counter. There was the sound of shuffling and faint laughter. More footsteps. They made their way through the hallway, four sets of shoes bringing dirt into the hallway of Mildred's home.

It was dark when they arrived in the bedroom. First the tall blonde boy with the red hat came in. He had his arm around a young girl with a bob of black hair. "God, Frank, you're such a creep," she said.

"You like it," Red Hat replied with slurred speech. The girl slipped into the bathroom while the other two sets of feet settled in the hallway.

Red Hat flicked his lighter at a cigarette hanging from his mouth and lit the room. In the flash of light, he caught a glimpse of my face and startled himself, falling backwards into the wall. The unlit cigarette clung to his dry lips.

"The fuck, Frank, be patient!" the girl called from the bathroom. A stream of urine splattered into the empty toilet.

"You're dead!" Red Hat yelled.

I said nothing.

"You're dead, bitch," he said again.

"Frank! Who the fuck are you talking to?" the girl called. She left the bathroom and entered the room.

"Oh shit!" she yelled when she saw my face. "I'm too stoned for this." She fell out of the room and stumbled into the couple in the hall.

"God, Jen, watch it," came Neck Tattoo's voice.

"C'mon, we're outta here," the girl said, and her footsteps ran with another pair of running legs out of the house.

"What's wrong with your girl?" Neck Tattoo asked as he entered the room. He caught a glimpse of me and toppled into Red Hat. Both boys pressed their backs against the wall and slid down to their behinds. Red Hat flicked his lighter again and held it at arms length, pointing it at me like some kind of weaponized crucifix.

"You're not real, man. You're not real," Neck Tattoo muttered to himself.

I said nothing.

"Listen, lady, we din't mean nothin'! It was an accident. It was all an accident," Red Hat yelled from behind his lighter. His words slurred and trailed off.

I said nothing.

"You're not real, man!" Neck Tattoo said again, pressing his back harder into the wall, trying to rise to his feet.

I walked towards him with the syringe from the bed in my hand.

"You're not real," Neck Tattoo repeated, this time beginning to cry. Red Hat, meanwhile, crawled backwards with wide eyes into the corner of the room and onto the mattress.

I approached Neck Tattoo, placing my left hand over his mouth and brought the syringe to his left eye. He let out a muffled scream from under my hand as I pressed it into him – through his eye and into his brain. Neck Tattoo fell to the ground moaning like a zombie. It was at this time that Red Hat began to scream.

When most people are about to endure something terrible, they release several short screams. They shriek in succession as if they mean to say words, but just can't find them. Not Red Hat. Red Hat just let out one long howling scream as I labored my way towards him.

Of all of the personal belongings I found left behind in Mildred's home, the most important of them was Mother's paddle. Its weight and heft felt good in my hand. I raised it in the air and paused in triumph before bringing it down on Red Hat's head.

Revenge was not swift. It was long and bittersweet. Red Hat's hands managed to deflect the first couple of swings, knocking his fingers in different permanent directions and spurring me to doubt my ability to make it past his waving arms. It was then, in the moment of my hesitation – the raised paddle held high and ready – that she came back to me. Beyond miles upon miles of ocean and worlds apart, her hand was my hand and my hand was hers once more. Together, we brought the paddle down, mashing his hair into the fragments of his skull and brain, sounding the beat of that glorious bloated thud that only Mildred knew how to play, and I danced again.

WHAT HAPPENED

His wife named her Lydia after Winona Ryder's character from "Beetlejuice," and it was a decision they arrived at during their last private conversation. She passed away during the birth of their daughter – their first and only child – and many said that it seemed as if he himself may have died with her. But, his spirit had been gone long before that, and what is a man without spirit if not dead?

The delivery was something that his deceased wife's doctors would label a tragedy, and it was something he would later only ever refer to as *what happened*. He packed those words and placed them neatly at the start of every explanation he would give to family and friends who waited for news with excitement that soured into condolences.

The words themselves, whether he vocalized them or wrote them down, always seemed to pull a vacant look over his eyes. "*What happened* was…" he would begin, then it felt as if the ground turned to quicksand. He would sink into an ankle-deep light sleep, his mind on a road trip to anywhere but here.

In the privacy of his home, *what happened* was not followed by any of the words his doctors gave to him –

15

obstetrical hemorrhage, uterine rupture, myometrial wall. Instead, a question mark followed, and he would tether himself to it and sink with it.

Every man carries a briefcase of burdens, and his was extra heavy. At the border of sleep, he would unpack his briefcase, holding an event in his mind, rolling it over and studying it until sleep would take him. But, sleep was never restful. He was often haunted by dreams that he would forget upon waking – briefcase dreams.

The memory of the car ride to the hospital was filled with love and nervousness. But once they arrived, there was urgency, and then blood – endless waves of viscid blood that covered hospital sheets and tiled floor like spilled paint. The odor of it nestled itself in his lungs, and he would never be free of it. Something about that smell shut off his memory's video recorder.

Circumstances beyond Lydia's control robbed her of the warmth and love of a maternal caregiver; she could understand that. But, Lydia could not reconcile why she was also robbed of her father's love. Of course, her father did love her, although she believed he blamed her for the loss of his wife. She would never speak those words out loud to him or acknowledge them herself. But the spirit of those words were tangible and carried a weight with them, a weight which Lydia readily received and placed upon her back.

Just as Lydia's father could not remember *what happened*, Lydia's memory of her childhood was vague, as moments worthy of recording were sparse. Lydia made friends at school and embraced her teachers' affection, even when it tasted of sympathy. After the end-of-year hugs, she wore their gossip and whispers like a "kick me" sign taped to her back.

Lydia's father had always hoped for a girl like Winona Ryder's Lydia – artsy and off-beat. However, instead of photography and poetry, Lydia was drawn more to school science classes and playing with animals. During the summers of her childhood, she started caring for a stray cat who wandered into her backyard. She would often begin her summer mornings by leaving a bowl of fresh water and left-over dinner scraps on the patio. At the start of summer, it would sometimes take hours for him to arrive, but by the end of summer, he would be waiting for her.

She named him Nightlight for his black fur and yellow eyes, which peered out to her in a way that reminded her of her own nightlight plugged into the outlet next to her bedroom closet. Nightlight was cautious of her that first summer, only receiving food when Lydia was watching from a window, but he grew accustomed to her and would eventually allow himself to melt into her arms for afternoon naps.

Lydia learned a lot about cats that first summer with him. In addition to eating pieces of chicken, tuna, and turkey, he would chew on pieces of olive and cheese (pizza). And, sometimes, he would even lick leaves of lettuce that she left for him. Though, unlike cats in the cartoons she watched, he never cared much for milk. She reported all of this to her father and asked to bring Nightlight into the house; he was pretty much *her* cat anyway. But, her father quickly dismissed the idea as "crazy" and waved a hand in the air as if to wipe away any idea of it. In fact, he insisted she stopped feeding the cat altogether, saying it reminded him of a woman he once knew, and it scared him. Lydia found her father's eccentricities to be hard to follow, but she learned that it was best to play along as well as she could. None of his plans or proclamations ever seemed to amount to much anyway.

Years ago, her father woke up one summer morning with an epiphany. "We're going to sell the house and move north," he stated. "This area is just..." he diverted from his thought, "we just need a change of scenery. You'll see." It was the first time she saw him express something that resembled hope, but as they packed the car and spent a series of nights bouncing from one sad motel to another, they somehow found themselves back home – Lydia with her *kick me* sign, and her father with his briefcase. There had been other proclamations too. One summer, for example, her father declared, "Every room in this house will have a salt lamp." But, it seemed that all of his ideas that started with full batteries couldn't sustain a charge for long. This would apply to Nightlight too. She was sure of it.

As part of her new summer routines, which no longer included feeding Nightlight, she still napped with him and sometimes watched him play. Though, as she would describe to her friends at school, his play often left her feeling "a bit gross."

Small lizards were in abundance around her house, and when Nightlight picked one out to play with, he would crouch really low, wiggle his rear end, and then pounce! The fight could last up to an hour with Nightlight batting and biting at them. But, he never killed them – at least not in the fight itself. When he decided he had spent enough time feeling domesticated, he would leave in the later afternoon to do cat things, and Lydia would do her best to move the little guys to a safe place where they could rest and regrow a missing leg or tail. She often found their bodies later, after they had died of internal wounds. But, she never stopped believing that they would recover.

In addition to her routines with Nightlight, Lydia grew into something like a caretaker for her father. Just as her days began with her caring for Nightlight, they often ended with her placing a blanket over her dad as he drifted in and out of sleep on his recliner. She cleaned around the house because her father had stopped doing it himself. She learned to cook because he would not, and she took care of herself when she learned her father could not. She was not Tim Burton's Lydia; she was her own Lydia – and a wonderful one at that. But, throughout her childhood, it was as if a theater were set for a performance for which no tickets were sold and no audience ever came. That sentiment formed as rocks in each of her pockets.

As Lydia transitioned from childhood to adolescence, she never stopped loving her father – never even questioned it – but she learned to stop asking for the warmth, love, and security of a parent in return. On her twelfth birthday, her father gave her a Hallmark card signed "from Dad," for which she hugged him – and meant it – before leaving to spend the night with friends. It was odd that a daughter could learn to be affectionate without having affection modeled for her in her family, but her greater freedom in adolescence afforded her more opportunities to be around other families where affection was expressed, and she basked in it.

Seeing affection in other families encouraged her to believe that that kind of warmth could exist in her own family too. After all, Lydia did have brief moments of it from her father. And, in those moments, she had glimpses of the real relationship that she might have had with him in an alternate life, one where he was relieved of his burdens. The closest they ever came to sharing a real and warm bond came during the strangest night of her life.

2

Lydia surprised her father by coming home early from a sleepover. She opened the front door to their house and found him in his recliner watching TV in the dark; flashes from the screen lit the soft contours of his face while a narrator droned on about seventeen hundred refugees traveling to Miami from Havana every week in 1962. Her father had been sleeping and, for the first and perhaps only time she could remember, he awoke with something resembling a smile.

"I didn't mean to wake you," she said.

"What're you doing home?" he asked, still groggy from

coming out of his nap.

"I just wanted to come home," she replied quickly.

"Sure. OK," he said. Even without being in tune to his daughter on more than a rare occasion, he could sense some kind of distress in the way she was carrying herself – extra tough.

She dropped her sleeping bag and backpack and carefully took off her shoes, which had tracked in some dirt and sand from their front walkway. For whatever reason, her father turned his head far over his shoulder to watch her, and she wished he didn't.

At the sleepover, Lydia's friend Tammy called another girl from school – Arianna – to talk about Lydia. Unknown to Arianna, Lydia was in the same room as Tammy and listening in on another phone to eavesdrop on their conversation. When Tammy and Lydia usually did this, it was an opportunity to hear more about rumors being spread around school or to hear what someone (Arianna) *really* thinks about somebody else (Lydia). But, this particular conversation turned especially cruel.

Tammy said to Arianna, "I heard you don't like Lydia." She left the statement hanging, implying, *is that true?*

Arianna replied, "Yeah, she's just a dumb orphan, and nobody would even care if she died. I mean, if I were her mom, I'd be glad I was dead, and I'm surprised her dad hasn't killed himself."

Most adolescents would have been upset to hear something so hurtful, but this was devastating to Lydia. Arianna had somehow broken the surface level barrier and peered deep into Lydia to find a combination of her greatest fears: her mother would not like her or want to be her mother even if she were alive, and her father was going to kill himself, leaving her all alone.

Lydia's father would not ever be described by anybody as doing well. Even before he lost his wife, he had lost his sister, mother, and father far before their time. His sister died in a car accident – hit by a drunk driver. His mother had developed a rare blood disorder that took her life, and his father passed away in a freak accident when he fell off the roof of his home. He attended many funerals and wished to attend his own, but it seemed as if his fate was to be a pallbearer, and not the man in the coffin. It drained him to bury his family, but even worse was the stigma that surviving friends and family attached to him, as if he were spoiled goods or a magnet for bad things. Even so, *suicide*? Lydia hoped *that* was out of his reach.

Lydia walked the long route back from Tammy's house and was glad for it. She needed to come down from the hurt and fear that had settled as a throbbing in her throat.

Her father interjected, "Hey, you want something to eat?"

She shook her head.

"There's some left-over pizza on the table," he encouraged. Images of missiles and missile launcher sites crossed the television screen.

Lydia picked at the dirt stuck on the sole of her shoe before getting up. She paused briefly, unsure of where to go or what to do before starting towards the kitchen. "Thanks," she said.

No, her house was never an emotionally warm place, but still there was something comforting about its smells and the knowing of where things were – even when they were out of place, or in this instance, in the dark.

As she moved into the kitchen, he returned his gaze to the television, and the narrator continued his monologue about the Cuban Refugee Program and people registering at the federal Cuban Refugee Center. Several short microwave beeps crept out in the distance, and Lydia's father pulled the lever on the side of his recliner to lift his legs. He was trying to remember what he was last dreaming about, but it escaped him.

His life had not been an easy one, and there was a sense of learned helplessness that he carried with him. He saw several therapists over the years, making efforts to unpack his memories. But, many of those sessions were spent avoiding the heart of the issue because, plainly, it was too hard for him. "What's the point anyway?" he would ask, shifting in his seat. "You can't change the past." And he was right; the physical reminders of worse times were always there. All of his meals were eaten off of his mother's fine china. His father's clothing lined his own closet. His sister's good luck charm had gone missing and left a dust-free ring on his nightstand where it once rested (another battery that lost its charge), and Lydia reminded him of his passed wife more than he would like. He had rid himself of his personal belongings on many occasions, but it seemed that no matter what, things had a way of coming back to him – just like that damned black cat in the backyard.

His thoughts were interrupted when Lydia returned with a glass of milk and a plate of pizza. She was at an age where her movements were in transition from childlike effort to the grace that comes with adulthood. Though, as she balanced her plate and simultaneously cleared a space for herself on the couch, she unknowingly stuck her tongue out of the side of her mouth – the universal image of a child in focus.

"Ah, so you were hungry," he said. She had his attention. Maybe it was something about the way she was carrying herself, or maybe it had to do with his brief recognition that she was not going to be a child much longer. And, if she weren't a child much longer, what might that mean to him? That he missed her childhood? That she's no longer a living reminder of *what happened*?

"Yeah," she said.

"You eat dinner there?"

"No, I didn't feel like it," she said coldly. Her sadness was beginning to hide itself under unfocused anger. She couldn't articulate the anger, but it was amorphously aimed at her father.

He pressed forward once more, "Why not?" He didn't

really care to know about whether or not she ate or why she didn't, but those questions were all he had to express a feeling that was beyond his awareness – that perhaps she in some ways reminded him of his wife, and some part of him remembered that she was his daughter, and he *did* love her. They were alone, the two of them, but he often felt as if they were never *alone* – always surrounded and haunted by the misfortune that followed him.

"I don't know," she replied. That was always good for stopping a conversation.

He replied with a nod of resignation and looked around his seat for the remote control but couldn't find it. Meanwhile, the narrator went on about President Kennedy imposing a quarantine on the importation of weapons into Cuba, for which Castro then prohibited transportation to and from Cuba. Together, father and daughter sat in quiet, with Lydia's occasional eating sounds filling the space between the show and commercials. When the program returned, the narrator reported on Oswald's murder of President Kennedy.

"Dad?"

"Hm?"

"Where were you when Kennedy got assassinated?"

"Hm," he groaned. The question seemed to catch him off guard. "Well, I was five years old, and I was in my kindergarten class." He thought about it further, "Yeah, the office secretary came in and announced that there had been a bad accident with Mr. Kennedy."

"But it wasn't an accident."

"No, no it wasn't. But I guess the school didn't want to be the one to break the news – not that they knew all the details then anyway."

"Were you sad?"

"Yeah, yeah I was sad about it. Mr. Kennedy was a good man. And, he didn't deserve *what happened*."

"Where was mom?"

"I don't know," he said with his gaze fixed on the TV.

Silence stood between them again, and the narrator continued about the deaths of thousands of Cuban refugees who illegally set out on unseaworthy rafts towards the United States. Her father seemed especially taken with this segment.

Lydia took strands of her long dark hair and began to weave them together. Her hair reminded her of a picture she had of her mother, and she wondered if she ever wore it in braids the same way. Her mind often made comparisons between her mom and herself, however brief. It was a strange sensation to long for someone you never met and would never meet. Since childhood, Lydia made lists of the questions she would ask her mom if she could, and then she would order them by importance, depending on how much time she might have with her in this imagined meeting between worlds. Tonight, there were too many questions to count or sort.

The narrator continued, "*President Lyndon Johnson's signing of the Immigration and Nationality Act of 1965 encouraged Cuban refugees to find asylum in the United States. At the same time, Castro made allowances for Cuban-born Americans to return to Cuba to pick up their relatives.*"

A look of disgust took residence on her father's face, and he leaned back with his eyes closed. His mind fixed on images of hands reaching out of ocean waters. A small snort escaped his throat, and Lydia looked over to see him nodding off. Another conversation crept into the forefront of her mind. Tammy had asked if Lydia's father ever took any pills. Lydia defended her father and firmly stated that he was not a drug addict (*and we're not going to talk about this further*), but doubt crept quietly in the back of her mind, setting cracks in the foundation of her beliefs about him.

The program went on, "*Combined, these two leaders were responsible for the unsafe travel of hundreds upon hundreds of refugees and their eventual drowning.*"

"That's sad too," Lydia said to herself, but loud enough to wake her father.

He looked at the television screen and saw images of rafts bouncing around the ocean. He muttered something under his breath.

"Do you remember when this was happening?" Lydia asked.

He paused and turned his head towards her on the couch and looked at her blankly. "I don't know," he said.

"Yeah, but you grew up in Florida. Do you remember it?"

He turned towards her again, this time with his whole body. His vacant look seemed to change, as if his batteries had finally charged – albeit briefly. He faced his daughter and stated again, "I don't know."

Lydia received the message: let it go.

3

Lydia's father awoke again when she covered him with the blanket that had fallen to the ground. He peeled his eyes open, saw her, and smiled. It had been a peculiar night as it was, with him being more sociable than usual, but this look he was giving her was unbefitting on him. She had seen it before – a look passed between her friends' parents, and sometimes she even received it from her teachers. It was a look of affection, and it had not been sprawled across his face in this way at any point that she could remember before. It struck her as cruel somehow – teasing.

Something was different about Lydia that night too; her sadness was intangible in a way that was novel for her. She was becoming a young woman, and she no longer carried her sadness like a child in tears or frowns, but she held it in her heart. Arianna's words echoed in her head, though she had choked them down well enough to let them sit in her gut beyond her awareness now.

"What are you looking at?" she asked. She didn't mean to come off as defensive, but it was too strange for her to be in the spotlight of her father's attention, and the light made her sweat.

"Why don't you come over here for a second?" He patted a place next to himself on the recliner. That dumb smile still holding his lips hostage.

Lydia glanced at him and felt an instant wave of resentment. It churned at her insides – fusing with the acid formed in her belly from Arianna's words. And yet, here he sat with a dopey look on his face as if someone had just whispered a grand secret into his ear. *Another poorly executed plan coming soon to a theater near you*, she thought. He patted the spot next to him again. "Come on."

"Who are you, and what have you done with my father?" she asked. "No, I'm not sitting over there." Lydia returned to the couch.

"Humor me," he insisted, and patted again.

She got up slowly, unsure of herself, similar to the way she watched her feet when she went to the beach, cautious to not step on any rocks or beached jellyfish. Was this Kodak moment meant to be for her or more for him, she wondered. She plopped herself down in her father's recliner, leaning forward and away from him. He lifted his arm and put it around her, and they sat that way uncomfortably for a few moments.

"I really had thought you would stay at your friend's house tonight, but I'm glad you're here," he said. In brief moments like these, he longed for the two of them to be closer, without the tragedies that stood as a wall between him and the rest of his life.

He was met with silence.

Her father let out a sigh and pulled a blanket over her with his free arm. In that moment, he was the father he could have been all along. He was a reactionary man, and his warmth that evening was a reaction to *something*, even if Lydia didn't know what it came from. But, he saw something in his daughter that resonated with him – an impalpable pain they had come to share.

In the way that the hands on a clock move without awareness of the gears that turn inside, he was going to progress forward, albeit entirely unaware of the forces that drove his decision. Nonetheless, he had made a decision, and he was a man of his word. He leaned back in his chair with her wrapped in his arm. Her face showed begrudging rebellion at first. But as time went on, she fell into a comfortable sleep, pressed into the sounds, smells, and feelings of a cozy Saturday night.

4

Lydia's father wasn't a bad man, he was just emotionally absent. And, when she awoke in the middle of the night, he had disappeared. The note she found was written just like him too – laying unceremoniously in plain sight and with inferences that he assumed someone else would understand.

> *Lydia –*
> *It is my hope that you won't see this note. In the case that you do, I wish your mother had the chance to know you. I wish I had the chance to know your mother with you, and I also wish that you had a chance to know me. I've never been the kind of father a girl needs, and in case you don't see me again, you've never been just any girl, and you don't need me – now or ever. I've never been good with words. I'm sorry.*

Lydia didn't dare call it a suicide note, because she couldn't think of her father in that light. That would hit her deep below the surface and would mean something about her and her worth – as a daughter, as a person.

It is my hope that you won't see this note. Lydia could only imagine what that might be in reference to. Her father was often a puzzle. He had said that her mom was a healing kind of person, and he was someone who needed to do a lot of healing – even Arianna knew that. Sure, she knew

27

her father mourned for her mother, always. But, if this was *the note* – the one she dreaded to find – well, what did he think would happen to it that would keep her from finding it?

The brain is a powerful organ, and it can work in mysterious ways to keep itself intact. So, while the disappearance (suicide) note of her father could have been a horrific and monumental discovery, it instead was just something that Lydia compartmentalized as an event that had happened or was about to happen. And similar to the lizards she tried to rescue from Nightlight, if she could help him, she would.

"Dad?!" she called out. She was met with silence throughout the house. She stood up from the recliner and turned off the television while moving to the kitchen in the dark. She turned on a light and called for him once more, "Dad?"

She moved into the hallway of the house and briefly considered the horror of finding him hanging from the ceiling. She shook off the image and checked the bathrooms, her bedroom, and his bedroom. A shoebox had laid on her father's bed, but it was empty. She hadn't seen the box before, but she figured that if it had held a gun, shooting it would have awakened her. As far as she could tell, she did not find any empty pill bottles, and he was not in the house.

With a sense of mild panic that was growing stronger, she returned to the kitchen and thought briefly about the note itself. She glanced around the kitchen and saw the block of butcher knives all sitting in their place. She moved past the kitchen table, bumping into it as she opened the sliding back door of the house. It was a windy night, and a gust of air pushed her back. She called for him in the darkness, "Dad?!"

The sound of her voice did not travel far in the wind. She quickly ran around the outside of the house and peered into their separated garage. The car was off and nothing looked suspicious. Next, she ran to the street and looked as far as she could in both directions – nothing.

I hate him, she thought to herself. Her anger brewing beneath the surface boiled up in pockets of hot air, begging for her to scream at him for having the audacity to kill himself and leave her alone – the nerve he had to think that she didn't need him, *now or ever*.

She ran to the back of their house and dodged a series of bushes as she left their property. Her bare feet scratched on the hard grass, and an occasional shell sent a sharp pain into the bottoms of her toes. It was about a half-mile to the beach, where she suspected he might be. She called out for him again, "Dad?!" Her voice still wouldn't carry in the wind.

Florida beaches are among the most photographed images in the world. The miles of sand, the bouncing blue waves, the image of a sun candidly caught on its rise over the horizon – they're pictures plastered across billboards and television commercials everywhere. But, a Florida beach looks different at night. She descended the boardwalk steps and shook her feet to loose the stray grains of sand caught between her toes. It was a silly effort before stepping onto the beach, but not a habit she could break.

During the day, the sand was razor hot. But, out of the sun's grasp, it was mild and cool to touch. She often came to the beach during her summer days, and her tan lines showed it. Though, this was her first time walking along the shore in the middle of the night. There was no laughter rolling in with the waves and no birdcalls or even distant music. Each wave poured over itself in its own crashing and then retreated. She called out again, "Dad?!"

The darkness of the night caught her by surprise. Any glimmer of moonlight that might reflect off the water was negated by heavy cloud cover, and the humming glow of surrounding community buildings seemed to fall off by the end of the boardwalk. Peering into the distance, the water and sky's horizon never met and never parted; they were one. It gave her an eerie feeling of being at the Earth's edge.

Lydia watched her feet as she made her way from dry sand to wet sand, being sure to look for beached jellyfish and sharp rocks. He was nowhere along the sandy shore. If he were, she might have been able to find him, but if he were in the water, he would be impossible to see. She wished she had thought to bring a flashlight.

The water threw itself at the sand and retreated. As Lydia approached, foam from the waves crawled over her toes and fell back, stealing traces of her body heat. A shiver ran up her legs and sent goose bumps down her arms. She screamed for him this time, "DAD?!"

She recognized where she was off of the coast and knew that just a little further down was the spot that her dad told her was where he had met her mother. She figured it was as good of a place as any to find him.

As Lydia ran in the ankle deep water towards the spot where her mom and dad supposedly met, she couldn't help but wonder if her mom had ever run along this beach at night. Was it possible that this was the same sand, or that their feet were running in the same waves, only decades apart?

He was nowhere to be found along the sand, but she did see a figure standing in the water in the distance. She ran to him, the ocean crashing against her shins and each wave pulling at the sand beneath her feet. Every now and again, a splash would send flakes of sea water to her lips that she would taste and morbidly wonder what it would be like to drown in that flavor.

"DAD!" she screamed from the water's edge. But, he was already waist-deep in the water and looking out over the ocean. He couldn't hear her calling from the shore. She splashed her way in after him, water spraying up and drenching her arms and legs. "DAD!" she screamed again.

The figure's shape turned towards her. She could make

it out from his silhouette that it was him, and he looked like he was carrying some kind of small bag. He wobbled with the waves that broke on him, struggling to maintain his stance.

"Lydia, what are you doing here?! Go home," he instructed. His batteries were charged again; she could see it in his eyes – his presence.

"Come back to shore! You're going to get sucked into the current!" Lydia shouted.

He didn't respond but continued to look in her direction. "You shouldn't be here," he cautioned. He was seeing her in a way that was new to him. And, for her, it was a new sense of being seen.

"Just come back here. Get out of the water!" she yelled again, unsure of what kind of mental breakdown happened to her father. There was something different about him – something immaterial, but did she dare think she liked this version more?

He paused again before responding to her, reaching into his bag to throw a mess of small things into the ocean. "Go home, Lydia. It's dangerous here," he called back. Again, he reached into the bag and threw something else into the crashing waves.

She took a step deeper into the water, wondering briefly if any dead Cuban refugees washed ashore at the spot where she stood. She tried to shake the thought and asked her father, "What are you doing out here?!"

He looked back at her and hesitated before redirecting his focus to his bag. Another wave struck him, shattering across his back and knocking him sideways.

Lydia took another step towards him, the water rising to her knees and crawling higher onto her legs. "What are you doing here?" she asked again in a softer voice. He stood still in the water several arm reaches away from her.

"This is where I met her, you know," he said.

A wave pushed Lydia backwards. "I know," she replied.

"And you look just like her, too," he said. He reached

31

out, his hand touching the edges of her hair that blew towards him. "I miss her."

"I know," she replied again. Another half step forward.

"But this wasn't the first time I was here," he continued. "I do remember the refugees."

"What?" she asked. "From the show?" She was face to face with him now and could see that the goofy smile from earlier in the night was gone. It was replaced with an expression of seriousness and authority, and it made her feel as if her father was a stranger.

"Yeah, from the show."

A wave knocked Lydia back.

"It wasn't sad like you think it was," he said with hopelessness in his voice. "It was sick."

Lydia looked at him with confusion.

"I saw them once, right here. This beach." He pointed into the water.

Lydia wrestled with maintaining her footing in the crashing waves. She could no longer see her feet or knees in the turbulent water.

"I was playing on the beach with a new pair of binoculars my dad gave me. I was looking out over the horizon and saw this raft," he started. "There must've been at least fifteen people on it, and there was a family in the water next to it. They were reaching up for them. The people on the raft wouldn't reach back, so the family in the water tugged at the sides of the boat and tried to get onto it, but they just couldn't. There was this man holding his baby, trying to swim, trying to get onto the raft," he paused. "His wife, I guess, too…" he trailed off. "Eventually it was just him in the water." A wave knocked her father forward again, this time bumping him into her and knocking her back.

Lydia imagined a picturesque Florida sun held proud in the sky over a tropical paradise with stretches of green and blue ocean as far as the eye could see, and beneath that, a turned boat with thirty arms and hands reaching helplessly out of the water.

"I was yelling to them, but I was all alone on the beach. Nobody could hear me. And the man, he climbed the raft and got on it. He just started killing them. He had some kind of knife or machete or something, and he just started hacking – *whack, whack, whack* – at each of them."

"My God," Lydia said with exasperation.

"They got him though. They overpowered him, turned his machete on him. They just hacked him to bits and kicked him over the edge. And, I guess the raft was too crowded because they started dumping a bunch of the bodies from the raft into the water. But, they weren't all dead. Some of them were still reaching up for the raft as it drifted away." Her father's voice cracked as he continued, "One by one, their heads sank below the water."

And how long, she wondered, would those bodies drift before they were found, or before they sank, or before they merely disintegrated and became part of the ocean themselves? Without any light, the water was a crawling shade of black. She squinted past her father and looked deeper over the water, looking for the horizon's edge through the darkness, but it was impossible to find. There truly was no beginning and no end to the ocean or the horizon. *They were combined, just like the drowned refugees in the water*, she thought.

"I stayed on the beach, watching," he went on. "I just didn't know what else to do. It must have been hours before the raft drifted to shore, and when it did, it was all covered in blood – *like spilled paint*. There were bodies laying all over it, and their guts were all mashed together," he explained.

"There was only one survivor, an old woman with a screaming baby," he said. "She was yelling something at me but I couldn't understand her. She just kept screaming, 'Llevar a mi hijo! Llevar a mi hijo!' She had lit these candles on the raft, and she was screaming at them and screaming at the baby. It was like a Santeria spell or something. And she kept screaming her head off at me at the same time, practically throwing the baby at me. I was just so scared! All of this blood kept coming out of her mouth while she was praying and crying. She was stabbed real bad, and I just froze!" He broke down in sobs.

"I couldn't reach for her. I couldn't do anything. And, I watched her like that – her pointing at me from the raft, bleeding to death, whispering at me until she died. 'Ojo por ojo, diente por un diente.' God, she had the scariest eyes, Lydia. It was like they could glow in the dark." He continued, "Lydia, she did something strange to me that day, and I don't think I've ever been the same."

"What about the baby?" Lydia asked.

"She drowned," he replied in his cracked voice. "I waited for her raft to drift ashore. And, when it did, I grabbed her! I got her." He hesitated before finishing, "But she was already dead."

"Oh dad," Lydia cried with her father.

"I would have buried her. I should have, but I was just a child!" He glanced at Lydia, his eyes tracing her face for judgment. The water knocked into him, and he fell to his side. "And I have buried her, but she always comes back!" He cried again, "I think this is the only way."

Lydia reached for his arm, "Let's get out of here! Come on." Her grip slipped off of him. The image of reaching hands yanked at her mind again. "We have to go!" she insisted.

"I took her home with me and…" he trailed off and stalled. "Go home, Lydia. I'm making it right. I have to make it right this time," he said. He returned his attention to the bag with him and turned towards the endless horizon.

Lydia pulled at his arm again, but it was no good. The water thrashed around him and rose. It was unlike anything she had ever seen. The ocean floor was falling out beneath him. "Dad, stop!" she screamed. The water rose above his neck and toppled over his head. "STOP!"

She followed after him, pulling at his arm once more, but she was still unable to get him out of the current that was pulling him further from shore. Another wave smashed into her side, disorienting her, and she lost sight of him as he went under.

Lydia thought to make her way back to shore for help and had turned from the ocean to the beach when a large wave hit the back of her knees, buckling them. It caught her by surprise, and she let out a mild shriek as her left knee crashed into a large rock of some kind, sending a wave of red pain up her leg. She grabbed at her knee and felt the ground where she had collapsed. It wasn't a rock she hit, it was something like a small rock sitting inside the bag her dad had been carrying.

She stood up realizing that there was no time to get help; she would have to find a way to pull him out of the water. She looked into the bag to see if there was anything in it that could help her – *a flashlight maybe*? In the darkness, she could hardly make out what she had. It felt like beads or marbles mixed into a bag with broken pencils. And then there was the thing that she struck her knee on that was *not* a rock. She pulled it from the back and saw a child's skull.

Lydia screamed and dropped the bag back into the water. Jumping into the waves on one leg, she tore into deeper waters, losing her footing entirely, as she reached and grabbed for her dad. Her hands waved past seaweed and small rocks stirred up by the waves. She frantically searched underwater for as long as she could before having to break for air. As she did, another wave crawled over her back, splashing water across her face. The sting of salt struck her eyes.

She ducked into the water again and reached for any sign of him. To her surprise, she felt an arm, but she lost it as she pulled. She dove deeper again, skimming against another limb that escaped her grasp. The thought of underwater creatures reaching out for her took her imagination.

Lydia emerged from the water gasping for air and treaded her legs to stay afloat. The violence of the water threw her backwards. As she turned her head from one wave, another slapped her ear with a ringing sound. Again, she was pushed backwards. In her panic, she could no longer identify up from down or left from right.

She held her breath and sank down to the ocean floor to spring up and break through the surface again for more air. In a moment of stability, she called for her father and found his body floating several feet beside her. *He's still alive. He has to be!*

As Lydia moved towards him, a dark figure rose from the water beyond him. From afar, it looked like a thin tree draped in seaweed ascending from the water. But as it moved closer, she saw exactly what it was: a creature with a skull face covered in decayed flesh and a web of hair. It approached her, steadily buoying towards her in the water, its long matted grey hair clinging to its disheveled features.

Lydia released a scream that tore at her vocal chords. A wave of water crashed at her open mouth, gagging her. While choking on water, she reached for her father, pulling him towards her and away from the corpse approaching them.

She was able to turn her father over so that his face looked towards the night sky. His skin was cool under her hands, and she kicked with all of her might to fight the current and to bring them back to shore. Her legs furiously splashed and kicked back at the thing following them.

Lydia fought against the weight of the water pouring over them and raced to bring her father's body ashore, but a string of heavy waves crashed over her and separated her from him. As the waves broke over them, Lydia was pulled into deeper waters while her father drifted closer to shore.

Lydia, amidst fits of crying and coughing, worked her way against the current to shallower waters without success. Another wave lashed across her back, sending her deeper into the horizon. Her knee throbbed in pain again.

Water slapped at her and disoriented her as she attempted to open her eyes through the burning salt water. The watching figure stood silent as the waves crashed and pulled at Lydia – taking her further from the shore.

A hand like a stiff rake gripped onto Lydia's shoulder. She threw her arm back to knock it off of her and managed to escape for a brief moment of clarity. But the respite of the waves was only a pause before another one made its crescendo and broke down over her body, slamming her head into the hard sand deep beneath her.

Lydia sprang from her legs again hoping to push off of something and felt the sharp stabbing pain where her knee had slammed into that skull. She was not going to make it to the surface.

As a second effort, she pulled her knees into her chest and grabbed ahold of her legs, hoping to float to the surface like her father had taught her to do. Her back rose and felt the soft lick of cool air whistling over her wet skin.

She reoriented herself and began to tread water, looking for the corpse woman around her. *Your father could have saved us.*

Lydia turned her head, briefly bobbing under waves that waxed and waned beside her. A panicked scream crawled its way up her throat, but never released in time to wake her father who was laying on his back on the sandy beach.

Another wave toppled over her head, turning her upside down. Just like before, she shot her legs straight out, hoping to hit the ground, but there was no ground for her. Instead, her right leg grazed something moving – something too firm to be a fish – something that was grasping at her.

Lydia waved her arms and legs about in a panic trying to breach the surface that must have been just a leg kick away. Coughing under water, she felt it again, something moving and this time touching her arm. It wiggled past her and wrapped itself around her forearm. In her bewilderment, she recognized it as a hand gripping her – this time soft and gooey, like a loose and melting rubber glove. A brief moment of hope filled her, as she believed she was being pulled to safety, when another hand wrapped itself around her ankle – this one hard and boney. Another hand pressed against her head. She was being pulled in one direction by all of them, building pressure within her ears and taking her from the torment of the waves thrashing across surface of the water, down into the cooler and calmer depths of the ocean. More hands grabbed a hold of her at her hips and shoulders and abdomen and neck as she made her descent. It was as if they were trying to climb off of her, like they believed they could push off of her and propel themselves to the surface.

The harder Lydia fought to remove the hands from her body, the more they seemed to reach out to grab at her. She swiped at them but found them too slippery to hold. Instead, her nails tore their old, decaying, and soggy skin from their bones. Alas, they refused to relinquish their grasp, and Lydia's protests of kicks and punches turned to gentle pushes as she lost her breath and fell into unconsciousness.

5

Ashore, her father choked on his own spit and vomit and seawater as he pulled himself from a restless sleep. He wondered if he dreamt Lydia being there with him or if she indeed was with him in the water. He often had strange dreams and struggled to know them from reality. But, something was different now, his briefcase was lighter.

The ocean continued to roll its waves – slower and less violently than before, calmed like a hunger that had been satiated. He sat up and wiped the hanging spit from his mouth with a cough. The bag he held onto for so many years was missing from him, and he felt tremendous relief for having finally rid himself of it – finally having returned it to the place from which it came. After all of his attempts to bury it, dump it, and burn it, it had always found its way back to him. He was hopeful that this time, returning it to the ocean, the woman who bled to death before him had finally found peace, having gotten what she wanted all of this time. He looked around himself again, and he truly was free of it. He let out a small chuckle as he fell back into the sand.

He thought of his wife and the night she passed away after hemorrhaging during Lydia's birth. It was a night of tragedy, but it somehow seemed to finally bury itself in the sand around him. His walls were broken down now, and for the first time in longer than he could remember, a sense of quiet and calm overcame him.

Dusting the sand from his pants, he turned towards home to tear up the note he left for Lydia. He would walk through the front door and find the recliner empty of her. He would search the house for her much the way she searched for him, examining every room for any sign or clue as to where she might have gone. The next day, a police report would be filed, and the following weeks would be spent actively searching for her. And, the rest of his life, he would be asking himself *what happened?*

BIRD'S THE WORD

His name was Bird, and he was a rather misshapen boy. He was thin and muscular, but boney – his body riddled with lumps from healed breaks and fractures from ill-timed and ill-fated jumps. In fact, that's how he earned his name; the goddamn kid was always trying to fly.

It started when he was two or three and took to the habit of jumping on his dad's bed. Once he got good at jumping on the bed, he started jumping off the bed. Then he started jumping from the stairs between the two levels of the house. It wasn't long before he jumped short and broke his ass on the bottom step. That didn't stop him from jumping though, just from doing it when his dad was home. He also tried a new experiment: jumping from the deck outside with an open umbrella. It didn't break his fall as well as he theorized. But, it did break his left wrist.

As a child, Bird spent more time in emergency rooms and doctors' offices than he would have liked. It was great fun getting his various casts signed by his classmates, but it wasn't worth it in the long run. They were too limiting. As far as Bird was concerned, aside from taking a leap off of something tall, the next best thing was the buzzing sound of the saw ripping through plaster and fiberglass, thus setting his limbs free.

Over the years, jumping for the sake of jumping escalated to extreme rollerblading, biking, and skateboarding. This probably wasn't the best hobby for the kid, given that he was careless and uncoordinated, but what else could he do? The joy of groundlessness couldn't be unlearned. His dad thought it was going to be the death of him – Bird, that is. But, that isn't ultimately what killed him. It wasn't even so much the carelessness or recklessness. In the end, it was his piss-ass attitude.

At about age fourteen, at the start of high school, he broke his pinky toe running into a lake when he failed to see a rock in his foot's way. It hurt like a bitch, but it healed. And, it healed on its own. He didn't even have to tell his dad about it, which saved him from the lecture that accompanied every drive to various medical facilities.

"You know I can't watch you every goddamn second. You need to think twice before you do the stupid things you do," his dad would start.

Bird would nod.

"Your mother would kill me if she were around to see what you've done to yourself."

Bird would sigh.

"I have to work, you know. I can't be driving to doctors' offices all the time."

Bird would taunt, "And you're not–"

"And I'm not a goddamn doctor either, you know."

Bird would shake his head. "And you work hard–"

"And I work hard to put food on your plate. I can't afford all these trips to the ER."

"Goddamn doctors," Bird would precipitate.

"Goddamn doctors making a fortune off me and your stupidity."

Bird would mouth the next word along with him, as if ending a sermon, "Goddamn."

So, Bird stopped going to the ER or the goddamn doctors, or to anybody, really. He broke ribs; they healed. He sprained ankles; they healed. And when he'd pop his shoulder out, another bone-busting friend of his – Eddie – would pop it back in. Fortunately, he saw it in a movie once. Eddie had a knack for that.

2

Eddie stood over Bird, watching the back of his head bleed from a hard collision with the ground. Eddie called to him as he brushed his hand over Bird's face and chest, wiping away a horde of bugs.

"Bird, come on! Wake up, man!" Eddie screamed and slapped Bird across the face. Gradually, as if turning the dials on a radio searching for a clear signal, Bird's eyes opened.

"What happened?" Bird asked.

"Your dumbass climbing abilities happened," Eddie responded while pointing up to the ledge from which they came.

"What?" Bird asked. Darkness surrounded them. A few feet away, a seizing flashlight pointed into the distance and a sprinkling of light came through a few small holes in a door about fifty feet above them. Slowly, as the radio transistor found its signal, everything started to come back to him.

3

It was the start of summer, and the two of them took a road trip to Texas to explore some caves. It sounded like a cool enough thing to do, and it was a good way for them to try to recapture the magic they had in childhood. They grew up as neighbors, living just a few houses away from one another, but sometimes it takes more than proximity to stay close.

They made it to Texas without a problem except for not having enough money to go caving with a group. That was OK, though, because Eddie knew about *these* caves.

He had seen something about them in a movie once, and no tour group was going to explore these caves anyway.

It seemed like Eddie was always coming up with some kind of lofty idea that he would try to sell to Bird. Most of his ideas were killed before they could take form. But, this one – this idea of going underground to explore some place that was only rumored to be in existence, well this idea had some traction to it.

Eddie pulled the car off the road and plowed through a wall of high grass. Bird looked over his shoulder to see the road disappear. The car shuddered as it moved, rattling their heads as they made their way over uneven ground. Bird was intrigued until Eddie pulled up onto a nubbin of dirt and parked the car.

"So what's with this place?" Bird asked. He took in the scenery, which included fields of high grass, mud, and trees as far as the eye could see. "Doesn't look all mystical and shit like you said."

"Just trust me, asshole," Eddie returned.

They exited the car, and Bird placed his foot into a deep pool of mud. "Great," he said. "Is this it?"

"I've never seen this place," Eddie replied as he slammed the driver's side door. "I just followed the GPS coordinates." Eddie looked around, there was no real clear path of where to go.

"What are you talking about?" Bird pulled out his phone but saw that he had no service. "Of course there's no service here," he muttered.

"Better leave that in the car," Eddie instructed. "This place is supposed to do weird things to tech stuff."

"Whatever." Bird tossed his phone through the car window and back onto the passenger seat. "Going to lock it?"

"No one else is out here," Eddie replied. He put his hand to his forehead to shield his eyes from the sun and scanned the tree line ahead of them. "This way." Eddie pointed towards a tree with a large white rock in front if it.

Bird pulled his foot from the mud, surprised by how much of a grip it had on him. Eddie, meanwhile, picked up a large stick on the ground and used it to part the grass over the dirt path in front of them.

"So, how are we supposed to find this place?" Bird asked, lunging his feet to dodge mud puddles.

"Just follow the markers – the white rocks. It's not too far from here," Eddie replied, stepping over an ant pile. "Listen, this is uncharted shit here."

"Sure it is," Bird chirped.

"You ever hear of Rockwall?" Eddie asked.

"No. Is that some town or something?" Bird returned.

"Yeah. It's a suburb of Dallas. You know how it got its name?" Eddie continued.

"No, I'm from Louisiana. Dipshit," Bird said while dodging tree branches. A spider landed on his shoulder, and he brushed it onto the ground.

"Well, back in the mid-1800s, some guys were digging for water and stumbled upon this giant rock wall that was buried underground. It's just like it sounds: a giant wall deep underground. And when they uncovered it, they also found a giant skull," Eddie explained.

"OK, but this isn't Rockwall," Bird quipped, wiping a spider web from his shoulder.

"You don't understand. They found all sorts of pictographs on it – like hieroglyphics – and maybe archways. All sorts of metal. They say it might be the marker of an antediluvian civilization."

"Anti-dildo-what, mother fucker?" Bird asked.

"Antediluvian – like, people before Noah's ark and the biblical floods," Eddie explained, stepping over a fallen tree.

"Even you don't believe that shit," Bird said while following Eddie's footprints in the mud.

"Maybe not literally," Eddie defended. "But, as historical record, all cultures across the world have legendary stories of giant floods wiping away civilization."

"OK, but this isn't Rockwall," Bird said.

"But, this might be *another* Rockwall," Eddie replied. "That way," he said pointing towards a small clearing between trees.

"Says who?" Bird asked.

"It's kinda just this rumor on the dark web," Eddie explained. "Some years ago, these two guys went hiking through here and found a metal door embedded in the side of a mountain. There was some abandoned construction and archaeology stuff that they stole and sold – like, some real deal equipment."

"OK? So now some group of Internet trolls think there's an ancient civilization there?" Bird scoffed, scraping mud off of his boot on the side of a tree.

"Well, get this. The whole reason these guys decided to hike through here in the first place is because they were driving through at night and thought they saw some lights out here. They said they thought they heard some screaming or something and wanted to wait to come back to check it out in the light of day. When they made their way through here the next day, all of that gear was left sitting there. They didn't find any bodies or anything." Eddie paused, "But they didn't open the door either."

"If there's really something there, wouldn't the feds or archeologists or whatever come back to it – like an investigation or something?" Bird asked and swiped at a mosquito on his leg.

"I don't know. But that's why we don't know more about Rockwall either. It all got called off and all further investigations got shut down. Officially, the wall is just 'geographic formations.'"

Eddie pointed to another white rock and crossed his way into the clearing, leading to a rusted metal door housed in the side of a mountain-like wall. For some reason beyond his understanding, it made his stomach drop. "Geographic formations my ass."

4

Under Eddie's direction, they found their way to their destination, unidentifiable by any kind of remarkable entrance. Off the dirt road, past a few mosquito-infested trees, hills, and turning paths, they found themselves in front of a browned metal door with a "no entry" sign. It led into something that appeared to be a wall. Bird was the first to try the door; it was locked. Bird shrugged and looked at Eddie. Eddie had a grin on his face and pulled a screwdriver out of his back pocket. Bird slapped at a mosquito on Eddie's back.

"Watch," Eddie said. He began to unscrew the sign from the door.

"Kind of a lame souvenir if you ask me," Bird said as he watched Eddie work at it. "Goddamn mosquitoes," Bird muttered and slapped another one resting on his forearm, smearing its body over his skin.

"Get excited," Eddie said with a smile. "We're going underground." He unscrewed the third of four screws. As the sign became unhinged, he pushed it aside and revealed a rusted out rectangular hole. Eddie reached his arm through, grabbed something, and screamed.

"What?" Bird asked solemnly, refusing to give in.

"Ah, nothing," Eddie replied with a grin. He moved his arm suddenly and opened his eyes wide as the door clicked open.

"Saw it in a movie?"

"Saw it in a movie."

Eddie waited for Bird to walk through and then closed the door behind them, allowing the sign to fall back into place. The door slammed shut with a thud. Using the small amount of light that peaked through the screw holes, Eddie relocked the door with a mock evil laugh.

"Nice touch," Bird quipped, and slapped at a bug crawling across his shoulder. They looked around where they stood, but it was really nothing to see. The three small holes in the door shot light into the dark like lasers and reflected dust, but failed to really illuminate much of anything in the blackness.

"All right, enough standing around. Take out your flashlight and let's head down. There should be a ladder here somewhere," Eddie directed.

They pulled out the flashlights that they bought at a gas station a hundred miles back and pointed them at the cave walls. They were jagged at the corners – sharp peaks – but very smooth overall and damp looking. What was unremarkable outside was compensated for in magnitude of size inside. The place was cavernous, and it seemed impossible to judge how far it went in any direction. They clung by the door, each of them having a private moment of wishing the other might chicken out. Alas, you can't go back; that's always been the central rule of their games.

"Found it," Bird said. He pointed his light off into the distance. The cave acted as sound vacuum, seeming to soak up his voice rather than echoing it the way he expected it would. Amidst the brown and orange ground, laid over with small rocks, puddles, and crawling things, there was a dull and decrepit ladder bolted into the stone. Eddie whipped around and shined his light on the ladder. As he did, the light shorted out.

"Oh, come on!" Eddie yelled and slammed his palm into the flashlight. "I just put in fresh batteries!" His voice didn't echo.

"It's fine. We still got mine," Bird replied, resentful that he had the one working flashlight. He slapped another crawling thing on his knee. "Man, I thought nothing was supposed to live in caves."

"Deeper in. We're still at the entrance," Eddie explained, still hitting his palm into the light. The bulb flickered before shorting out again.

"Well, I'm getting sick of these bugs, so let's get on with it," Bird said with impatience. Once he approached the ladder, he put the flashlight in his back pocket and started his way down. It was cold in his hands.

There was an occasional lightning strike of Eddie's flashlight above him, as Bird went rung by rung down the ladder. As he made his way, he tried to remember how many rungs it took him to make it onto the roof of his house. This was certainly more than that, but how many times more than that? Two? Three? He didn't want to admit it to Eddie, and he could barely even admit it to himself, but there was something uncomfortable about this place. As he approached the bottom rungs, something crawled – no, slithered – across his hand. He instinctively let go at the same time one of his feet slipped, and that was it: off to that world of dreamless sleep.

5

"You will feed me," Bird muttered under his breath as he came to.

Eddie laughed with relief. "Jee-zuz! What the hell? I thought you died."

"Can't kill the birdman," Bird replied slyly. *Or can you?*

"I was messing with my light and you 'kerplunked' like out of those old Looney Toon cartoons."

"You watch too much TV," Bird replied absently while rubbing his stinging face. He gave Eddie a questionable look. "Did you hit me?"

"I had too. You were out cold," Eddie explained.

Bird laid still and did a status report on his body. His ankles were fine. His legs were fine. His ass hurt, but that was nothing like when he broke it. His back throbbed, but it was OK. His shoulders were in place. His arms were fine. His neck was fine, except for a numb throbbing on the right side. His head hurt, but it wasn't fatal. He wiggled his fingers and toes cautiously as he had done a million times before. "I think I fell off the ladder," he muttered.

"You think?!" Eddie sighed and laughed again, this time with real relief.

"How far down are we?" Bird asked.

"I don't know. It's really hard to tell," Eddie said, taken aback by their depth into this place. He figured Bird's fall was enough to put an end to the trip and was relieved for it. He moved the light to their surroundings and couldn't even find the walls of the cave. They appeared to be in an endless tomb of darkness, minus the cold and wet dirt at their feet.

Eddie shined Bird's flashlight across Bird, wiping furiously at some creepy crawlers on his chest. "Let's get you up and out of here," Eddie suggested. "This place is infested with bugs."

"I'm fine," Bird replied as he sat up slowly, pushing away Eddie's hand. But, damn, did his head hurt. His brain felt like a ship in a bottle that was slammed against the sides a few times during a storm.

Eddie helped him up regardless of his resistance, and they sat together for a while in the dark before Bird thought he could climb back up the ladder. "So, you're hungry?" Eddie asked.

"What? No. Can you turn off that flashlight? My eyes, man."

"Yeah, yeah." Eddie shut off the light. "You gonna be all right?" Eddie asked. They sat in greater dark.

"I'm not dead."

"Yeah, but you could have a concussion."

"Whatever doc, I'm fine."

"Shut up. Just make sure you don't hit your head on the way out."

As the lasers piercing the door above lost their intensity with the descending sun outside, Bird finally felt strong enough to make his way up the ladder and through the path of sporadically placed white rocks to the car. Eddie was behind him the whole way making sure he made it.

Once they arrived at the car, it was decided that they ought to cut their trip short entirely and head back home. Well, it was decided by Eddie. Bird didn't want to be accused of being a pansy, so he refused to go home. There were antediluvian skulls to find, after all. But, it was Eddie's car, and it took him wherever he wanted to go.

"How's your vision and everything?" Eddie asked with concern as he piloted them down the road.

"We didn't have to turn back, you know," Bird replied, continuing his show of toughness. His head hurt like hell, but what really bothered him were the damned spider bites – or whatever bites they were – that ran across his arms. Even worse than those, though, was the numbing bite he had on his neck. Whatever did that must've had fangs.

The trip was really something like the end of an era for the two of them. The school year finished, and Eddie would soon go off with his family to their vacation home on the East Coast while Bird worked menial jobs back home for little above minimum wage. The magic that remained in their relationship would be gone. They would start the summer by sending a couple of text messages back and forth as they always did – but the amount of time between each response would grow until they were no longer sending them.

Eddie liked to look forward to the excitement of the future, while Bird liked to look backwards at how good things used to be. Even when they hadn't actually been that good, Bird found a way to make himself believe that they had. In the end, they wouldn't follow their projected trajectory to decrescendo towards being nothing more than acquaintances when Eddie ultimately left for college. And, it wasn't a girl that would end their friendship like each of them privately thought might happen. No. Instead, Bird was going to die in a few days.

"Can I stop to get you some aspirin?" Eddie asked. "Actually, that might be bad if you have a hemorrhage. Isn't aspirin a blood thinner?" Eddie asked rhetorically. He turned to Bird and glanced at his face. "Eh, your eyes aren't dilated," he said.

"I'm fine, man," Bird cut in. His head buzzed, but he

didn't think it was from the fall.

Eddie fell silent.

"It's not even my head, really. These spider bites, or whatever, they itch like crazy. Especially this one," Bird said and pointed a finger to his neck.

Eddie took his eyes from the road to look at Bird's arm. "Those will go away, just need a little steroid cream," he said. He looked at the one on Bird's neck. "But that..." Eddie shook his head, as if he could shake off what he was seeing.

"What?" Bird asked and pulled down the passenger side mirror. "Oh—"

"Well, that'll make you forget about your head," Eddie quipped and returned his attention to the road.

It did. Bird's head, other than being a little achy, was fine. His vision was normal. He didn't need to keep worrying about it. On his neck, though, right under his jaw on his right side was something like a marble under his skin with a red dot in the center of it. It was solid, firm to the touch, and it felt dry like a callous had grown over it.

"Might want to keep an eye on that," Eddie suggested. The look of the thing – its bulbous contours – made his stomach turn.

"Yeah," Bird replied under his breath and squirmed to get a better view of it in the mirror. He squeezed it gently between two fingers. It burned and brought his body to a mild sweat.

"But watching it isn't going to help," Eddie said. He reached over and closed Bird's mirror.

"It itches," Bird shot back as he scratched at it. He stopped as the burning began again. It radiated out of the marble and up and down his neck and into the base of his jaw. He sat on his hands. Eddie fiddled with the radio. There wasn't much for them to talk about in the wake of their failed expedition, and it was going to be a long drive home. Bird followed the dashed lines of the highway with his eyes and fell asleep.

6

Bird hovered over his body plastered on the ground of the cave that he had met with such force seconds before. Where there had been only darkness, he could now see himself stretched out and made damp by the puddle of water he was lying in. Yet, he wasn't lying in it, he was standing over himself.

Small creatures with many legs and antennae searched his corpse, taking inventory of what they found. Long crawling millipedes and centipedes thicker than snakes wrapped themselves around his arms and weaved themselves between his splayed fingers.

In the distance, Eddie shook his light from the top of the ladder, muttering to himself as he worked to find his way down into the cave. *Am I dead?* Bird wondered. *Is that what this is?*

In the darkness around him, he knew he was not alone. The cave trembled with vibrations running across the walls and ground.

From above himself, he scanned his body, which was not a corpse as he had thought; his chest still moved faintly. And somehow, in this dream he could hear now what he could not hear before: the sound of pulsations, as if the air itself were breathing.

With his disembodied sight, he found that he and his friend were at the opening of what appeared to be an infinitely deep and contorting cave. And he could feel now what he could not feel before, that there was life in that cave with them – an energy that radiated and grew stronger from deeper within the cave itself.

His gaze spanned towards Eddie steadily making his way down the ladder towards his own body flattened on the ground. His gaze stopped there, again looking at himself with a sense of longing that was foreign to him, wishing to be back in his vessel. Alas, he was equally compelled to wander deeper into the cave. A collection of quiet whispers summoned him towards the infinite blackness that pulsed with life and death.

As if led by a magnetic force, his disembodied-self stumbled further away from his shell of a body, first slowly, then rapidly, moving deeper into darkness.

Amidst the black, he found he could see without light. In his vision he found etchings and carvings in the cave walls. Crude images of giants slaughtering beasts marked the slabs of stone, all with bones and freshly-bloodied animal remains at their bases.

Echoing from behind him, the sound of a slap chased its way to Bird's disembodied ears and pulled him back into his body.

7

By the time Eddie's car pulled into the driveway of Bird's house, the sun was beginning to rise – its brightness an offense to Bird's dilated pupils.

"Hey, let me know how you're doing tomorrow. Maybe come up with a name for the thing on your neck, too," Eddie said with a forced smile.

"Yeah, yeah," Bird mumbled in return.

"And maybe get that thing checked out," Eddie continued. "Seriously."

"Enjoy your trip," Bird replied, and closed the car door. He walked into his house with the rising sun at his back. The worst hangovers of his life could not touch the amount of sick he felt. He held his aching head in his hands as he attempted to make his way up the stairs to his bedroom. Each step seemed to send a shockwave of pain around globe of his skull and a wave of nausea to his gut. The walk from the hallway to his bedroom felt like an eternity. Finally approaching his room, he collapsed onto his bed with sounds of millipedes and centipedes writhing in his ears.

8

There was a knocking at Bird's bedroom door. He peeled an eye open and made a groaning sound in the direction of the door, catching a glimpse of the digital clock on his nightstand. *Seven o'clock? How long have I been out?* Bird thought to himself. *Two hours? Fourteen hours?*

"Hey, you in there?" his father yelled from the other side of the door. The knocking continued. "Time to getcher grub."

Bird swiped at the clock on his nightstand, sending it to the floor with a bang. "I'm coming," he shot back.

"Goddamn kid." The words hung at the door as his father's footsteps walked way.

After Bird's internal radio caught a frequency, he stumbled his way down to the dinner table where a grilled slab of meat laid on a plate with potatoes. Bird scratched at his neck. It burned and turned his appetite. Following the same head-in-hands walk of shame as before, he returned to his bedroom without eating.

"Maybe lay off the dope!" his father called up after him. And not before Bird fell back to sleep, his father finished under his breath, "Worthless sack of shit."

9

Bird found himself again on the ground of the long contorted cave as before. Above him, occasional slices of light danced as Eddie shook his flashlight. Bird could sit up now, but noticed that he sat up without his body.

How badly he ached to be back within himself so that he could roll-over and run out of this wretched place. He thought to lie back in his body, but to do so, he would have to sink into it amidst the sea of flaccid bodies and legs climbing over him.

He began to notice again the quiet sense of presence in the cave, reminded that he and Eddie were not alone.

Once more, the presence in the cave called to him in a harsh language of whispers.

Bird drifted away from his body like before, moving towards the grand blackness of the cave's depths. As he crept further from himself, he noticed more etchings of giants carved into the stone walls like a crude prehistoric art gallery. They presented giant men hunting creatures, but the bodies of their sacrifices were shared not amongst the giants; they were laid before their god – a horrific insect-like beast that consumed their bodies. The giants, too, were sacrifices to the insect-god.

10

By the time Bird awoke the following morning, his father was already at work. Flushed with fever, he bent over and vomited along the side of his bed. Sitting up was an act of labor, and his body left a puddle of sweat on his uncovered mattress.

Stumbling with one eye open, Bird made his way to the bathroom where he began examining his neck. The marble under his jaw had grown to the size of a golf ball. The skin over it had stretched to accommodate the lump and peeled off in dead layers. It was tender to the touch, but more numb than sensitive, for which Bird was relieved. Nonetheless, when he touched it, a dull thudding pain throbbed and moved up his jaw. It made it hurt to groan. And when the lump began to move, Bird lost consciousness.

11

Bird found himself standing at a great hollow auditorium in the cave, surrounded by vast emptiness but for the cold and damp ground beneath him. The whispers spoke with hostility, biting at him in countless tongues. Here, it was made known to him that he was in the tomb of the Great

God of All That Crawls: the spirit of the God of Decomposition – He Who Feeds on Giants. "And you will feed me," It commanded.

An enormous creature with a shell body and pinchers perched atop an endless bed of legs worked its way towards him. It raised itself over him, with worms and slime pouring from its mouthparts, its mandibles and other organic machinery designed to tear at flesh. "All who come before me will be consumed, and you will feed me," It proclaimed.

Bird looked to where his feet should have been but could not find them under long, thick black worms crawling their way up his legs. He stumbled backwards and fell into the pool of twisting worms and centipedes, sinking into them as they wrapped themselves around his body. In his terror, a slap echoed throughout the cave that yanked Bird back through to the mouth of the cave and into his body.

12

"I'm taking you to a doctor," Bird's dad stated. He stood over Bird, his hand raised and ready to slap him to wakefulness again.

"I'm fine," Bird spit between his locked teeth. He was soaked in sweat, shivering and burning.

"Look at you. What in God's name did you do to your neck?" his dad asked.

"Nothing."

"If your mother was alive…"

"But she's not," Bird interjected. His words sprang from his lips with spittle.

A dull, blank face overtook his dad's expression. "Goddamn kid. Can't afford no more goddamn doctors anyways." He rose to his feet and walked away, leaving Bird to crawl on his hands up to the sink where he pulled himself up – his face peering over the edge of the bathroom counter. He was pale and wet.

He slowly raised a hand to touch the egg-sized tumor in his neck and recoiled at its sensitivity. His eyelids opened and closed slowly. He vaguely remembered thinking that he saw it wiggle and cringed at the thought of it. After splashing some water on his face and drinking from the sink, he made his way back to his bedroom.

As he sat at the edge of his bed next to a puddle of vomit, his internal radio began to lose frequency, the messages became less clear. His fever was growing in tandem with his robust neck. The lump was becoming more painful, and pulsated with its increasing size. The dial turned to static, and Bird was out.

13

It's alive. That was it; whatever was growing inside his neck was alive. He was awake now – awake and sharp – his thoughts at their clearest since the fall. No, clearer since even before he hit his head, before some goddamn creature raped his neck at the bottom of that ladder.

If it's alive, I can kill it. I'll free it, and then kill it. Kill the goddamn thing.

He sat upright, moving fast, having to move while the radio played. He reached into the drawer by his bedside and pulled out his pocketknife and lighter.

Free it and kill it. If it's alive.

His fever broke, and he felt good – the best he had since that fucking cave and his visions of some deformed god of bugs. He ran to the bathroom, stumbling over piles of laundry sprawled across the floor. There was urgency – this had to be done, and it had to be now. Now, before the signal falls back to static.

Free it. Kill it. If it's alive.

His hand groped for the bathroom light in the dark. Once he found it, his thinned face and sunken eyes glanced back at him from the mirror, and for a split second, he feared he was not himself. *You will feed me.*

The skin over the lump in his neck cracked like an eggshell.

It's alive. Free it. kill it.

His jaw ached and remained clenched, muscles tightening with every twitch made by the thing in his neck.

Free it. kill it.

He raised the pocket knife and held the blade in the flame of the lighter until its edges turned blue. Once the blade was deemed sterilized, he held it out in his hand, watching his reflection in the mirror move with inverted precision. *You will feed me.*

He slowly brought the knife closer to it, carefully moving his hand forward and backward trying to make the image in the mirror match what he needed his body to do. He brought the knife tip to the edge of the growth.

Free it. kill it. You will feed me.

He took a deep breath and stabbed in. The blade cut through the surface of his neck and into a green mucus-like gel, coalesced with blood. He let out a scream as waves of incinerating pain jumped from the knife's tip throughout his body. The sharpness of it forced his hand open, leaving the knife embedded in his neck.

The ooze smelled of sulfur and ran down his body – warm and feverish. But Bird stood through the pain, long enough with the knife protruding from his neck to see a worm the thickness of his finger squirm its way out of the hole that was made and fall onto the bathroom counter.

The pain forced his clenched jaw open, and he screamed with all of his strength. Hijacked by his panic, Bird removed the knife from his neck, shooting a spray of blood across his reflection in the mirror with every beat of his pulse. *You will feed me.*

Amidst the rhythmic firing of his blood against the bathroom mirror, Bird focused all of his attention onto the knife in his hand and brought it down on the gray faceless thing slithering across the counter. It split in half with ease.

Bird hunched over the bathroom counter, bringing his face to the worm's level, its two halves moving in opposite directions. Again, in one last motion, Bird brought down the knife onto one of the halves, leaving three portioned pieces of the creature squirming in puddles of his own blood.

The radio faded fast – the broadcast quickly signing off and turning to static. As he lay dead, the three halves of worm above him slowed, stalled and bled. And, in the end, my friends, the surly Bird got the worm.

SHE SAID HER NAME WAS SPOOKIE

She slid a whisky sour down the counter and landed the glass firmly in my hand. *Touchdown.* "To your campaign," the bartender said with a sip of her own drink.

"Cheers. You ever run into any trouble, you know who to call," I returned as I lifted my drink with a smile.

I threw back the last few sips and took in one last glance of the room – some empty barstools and a few frat boys fighting over which of them was going to roofie the blonde. A few years ago, I'd have played too.

The door slammed itself in the wind as I bailed on the circle jerk that was about to happen behind me. It was the second scoreless night in a row in my new stomping grounds – still acquainting myself with city life, I guess.

I stepped out onto the street, taken aback by the cool night air. The wind whipped a band of browned leaves at my shoes with waves of soft and muffled conversation following. For as many people as there were in bars and restaurants for blocks, I somehow found myself alone and miserable with a string of parked cars.

It's funny how, in the same way one song might remind you of another, one unrelated and seemingly mundane thing can pluck you out of your world and drop you off in another. It's like time travel. Surviving something once isn't enough, you have to do it over and over again.

For me, that empty street was the high school parking lot on prom night. Just the same, the empty barstool next to me had been the lonely spot on the wall next to where I stood in the gym. Yeah, nights like these are all the same: a tease with their promise that they just might end differently. But, then they go on to confront you with the ugly truth that you really have nothing to offer anyone.

So, I guess that's how I made college different. You run from one world to the next, right? Well, in college, *I* made my own promises. 'Brian the Brain' was 'King of Nerds' no more, and I had the list to prove it. My number of conquests was legendary, and if it hadn't been for that legal thing that happened, I'd still be taking names.

I was starting down the block, simultaneously hailing a cab and fighting myself to go back to the bar to make a bid for the blonde – *lawyers be damned!* – when my luck on the night changed.

"Psst – over here," she whispered from the alleyway. At first, I thought I was hearing things. It was just me and the parked cars without a *her* to be seen. "Psst," she whispered again.

I looked over my shoulder and caught a glimpse of her hand revealed by shadows; her index finger urged me closer. "C'mere," she encouraged. Her long, white and slender fingers played imaginary strings in the air as they summoned me.

The moon lit the night well and unveiled her as I moved towards her. The reflected light contoured the corners of her face – smooth skin hidden under long layers of multi-colored hair in pigtails and dreadlocks. I was struck by the intensity in her eyes, made even more gripping by the eye shadow that surrounded them.

"Got a light?" she asked. Her lips pulled into a grin.

"I do," I replied and pulled a matchbook from my pocket. I quit smoking years ago, but I'll be damned, a smoker knows the value of hanging onto a spare book.

A burst of flame pulled the shadows from her, the bouncing light making her look as if she were about to tell the punch line to a horror story at a campfire. She wore some kind of corset halter-top thing that highlighted her arm sleeve tattoos; I could have sworn they were moving.

They say that a full moon brings out the crazies, that it creates a gravitational pull that stirs up the oceans and all the water on the planet. If people are mostly made of water, then that includes us too. I can tell you, my insides were stirring.

She brought a cigarette to her lips, and her eyes locked onto mine as I leaned forward to light it. "Thanks," she said in her whisper. Her words were framed with some accent I couldn't place, and she had an air of being, well, not from here. "Nice night?" she asked.

I nodded, hesitating before responding. Frankly – and embarrassingly – I was jarred by her beauty. In a better part of the city, she could have been a world-famous model. She had the long slender frame for it, but there was something tragic about her too; stepping into the alleyway with her was like standing in a mausoleum.

"Yeah, nice night," I conceded. "And for you?"

I couldn't make sense of our meeting – of her being alone in an alley without someone to light her cigarette for her. Any second, I expected a couple of thugs to hit me across the back with a bat or to pull a gun on me. Hell, maybe she already picked my pocket somehow; it felt like she picked my brain.

"Nice enough," she smiled, and I caught a different angle of her that showed a trail of eye shadow that had dripped, presumably with a tear. *Or did she draw it that way?*

"Those'll kill you, you know," I joked.

"Wouldn't that make you complicit?" she replied with a smirk and took a drag.

"What's your name?" I asked.

"They call me *Spookie*," she laughed and lunged at me

with a playful claw swipe. Her hand was covered by a fishnet glove and toy spiders dangling from stray threads. It was the first thing she said above a whisper, and it came with a roar.

"Oh yeah?" I jumped back with more of a startle response than I expected.

"Yeah," she laughed again and paused to look at me before dropping her cigarette to the ground. She crushed it under one boot and placed a piece of gum in her mouth.

"Just one drag?" I asked.

"I only take what I need," she smiled again, this time with all of her teeth. We stood without words again for a few brief seconds, like she was making some kind of assessment about me. "I get it, you're a shy boy, yeah?"

"Can I buy you a drink?" I asked. She turned and started walking deeper into the alley, looking at me over her shoulder to see that I was following. I was.

Whatever light the moon provided seemed to stay in the street. I could hardly see my feet in front of me, but I felt her hand reach back to touch mine. It was warm, and I swear it gave my stomach a feeling of falling that I haven't felt since, well, maybe ever.

"Follow me," she said. I would have followed her anywhere.

Let me tell you something; I don't believe in love. Now, that's not meant to be a secret confession or anything. But, I've never been in love. If ever there were such a thing as love though, it was being in her presence.

I followed her into the alley and through the backdoor of some building that looked like it should have been condemned decades ago. Beer cans and fast food bags crumpled under our feet as we rounded a spiral staircase that led us down what felt like an infinitely deep well.

Every few steps, discarded light sticks burnt their last embers under our steps, her boots working perfectly in synch with my Italian leathers. Every now and again, there was enough light to peak at her torn leggings that disappeared under a short skirt.

Towards the end of our vertical tunnel, thunderous drum beats and electronic dance music pushed back at us. Finally at the bottom, we were greeted by flashing green and purple strobe lights. A sea of dancers bounced ahead of us in stop-motion.

She looked back at me and mouthed something. It was impossible to hear, but there were dimples in her smile. She grabbed my hand again and weaved me through a crowd of dancers bobbing in rhythm to the music.

She faced me with a smirk and closed her eyes to the tribal hammering that shook the room. With our hands linked, she carved a space on the dance floor just for us. I surveyed the room as she knitted her body in her own darkness, the flashing lights unable to define her. She was lost in the music, and I was lost in watching her lose herself. She held her arms in the air and swayed her hips, each swing tossing her hair and her threaded spiders like shadows.

Songs faded into one another, and she moved like a snake to them all – coiling her way around me. I seemed frozen in space and time, breaking my gaze only to wonder if I was moving with her or if she was moving for both of us. She swam in the music, and I was her shore. It was the sensation of quenching a thirst I've had all of my lifetimes.

2

One afternoon when I was a little boy, I ruined the family room television when I set a bunch of magnetic toys on it. After an hour of yelling, my mom explained, "Magnets change the path of electrons and alter the firing of photons, Brian. When you leave a magnet in a certain spot on a TV for too long, it magnetizes that spot and permanently distorts the color there." Dancing with her was like a magnet to the brain – yellows, purples, and greens in all the wrong places.

We walked down a maze of streets and alleyways with our hands clasped together. The moon seemed to set, and fall, and rise again, matching my own sensation of falling upside-down inside. Sometimes, I felt as if I were floating, her delicate hand being the only thing keeping me from drifting into the sky. Other times, I was walking, and she was floating.

I remembered my address well enough to guide us there. My eyes locked with hers, and we seemed to move down a river current towards home.

3

Through dizzying vision, I saw the ceiling of my apartment: support beams, vents, painted metal sheeting. She straddled herself across me, rocking her body, her hips swinging the way they danced – like a hypnotist's violent pendulum. She arched her back, rolling her head and staring at the mirror locked above us. As her reflected glance met mine, she smiled her toothy grin and ran her hands across her naked body. They were covered in blood.

4

I don't know how much time elapsed before I could open my eyes again. When I did, my bedroom's view of the city crept into focus. My lips quivered when I attempted to call her name. She was there, though; I could feel her presence in the sheets around me. In fact, I was moving – still rocking – but I could feel nothing. I was frozen, stuck inside my own body.

My head was locked to the left to stare indefinitely at the skyline from my bed. I jerked my eyes to the right but could not find her. My head was pressed to my pillow and would not move. With all of my might, I turned my head, climbing millimeters that felt like miles, to face the ceiling again. I shot my eyes open once more and found her in the shadows. A large ceiling fan cut the light into rhythmic flashes against her face. As she moved closer, her presence burned the magnet deeper into my brain, and my vision swirled.

"What's happening to me, Spookie?" I choked.

Her head moved next to mine, placing her breath in my ear. "Shhhh," she whispered. Deathly calm followed.

5

I awoke from dreams of suffocation. My eyes locked on the ceiling mirror again. Her body was no longer on mine, but a dark shape sat against the wall to my right. I heard shuffling as it made its way up the wall. "Spookie?" I uttered.

This time, there was silence. I turned my eyes towards her as much as I could and found a scaled creature with tentacles and an assortment of limbs pressed against the middle of the wall. She climbed towards the ceiling like a spider. *Photons, Brian.*

She settled in the corner between the wall and ceiling, a nest of limbs and wings squirming in her silhouette. "What are you doing to me?" I mouthed without sound. A pressure welled up in my head, and I closed my eyes.

6

When I awoke next, I was entirely immobile. Each breath I took was a conscious, labored movement in my chest. The room spun around me, and I knew she was close. I could smell myself on her in thick waves of iron. My eyes fluttered before opening, and in an instant, she was upon me. She was covered in streaks of blood, every part of her as hideous as she was once beautiful.

I attempted to move but was restrained by the weight of her pressing against me, rocking again with that awful pendulum swing of her hips. Her face pressed into mine with her mouth grinning against my cheek. Her texture was rough and hot. Under a wave of her humid breath, I turned my head and shut my eyes. A string of copper-flavored spit crept its way down my face, over my lips, and onto my neck.

The magnet returned to my brain, and I felt like I was falling into a pit inside my own body. It was the sensation of being pulled out of myself. As I trembled in her clutches, she released something like a growl. I wished with all of my might to get up and run, but she was immovable. A whimper escaped me as I fell into unconsciousness.

7

I awoke to the sensation of my right leg being fed to a wood chipper. I opened my eyes and saw that it was in her mouth, having chewed her way past my knee cap. Her lips rested on my thigh as she moved her head rhythmically, sawing away at it. Her jagged teeth were embedded into my flesh, mashing back and forth while her tongue whipped itself at the blood that poured from me.

Unable to control myself, I prepared to scream. As I inhaled, she raced across my body and pressed her mouth to mine, sucking the air from my lungs. I had no scream to give. The sound I made was lost in the coagulated blood that had pooled in my throat from her kiss.

8

I peeled my eyes open and broke the crusted seal of blood that crested over my eyelids. The room was crowded with more creatures like her – gendered beings in leathered robes with hooks and chains. Their faces were long and torn, straddling the line between beautiful and grotesque. My eyelids trembled as I struggled to find the strength to keep them open. I scanned my body in the ceiling mirror and saw that I was emaciated to near nothingness, having somehow lost my body mass over the course of the night. My ribs were skeletal and exposed, my skin translucent, and I watched the sporadic pump of my heart beat in my chest. My legs and arms were gone.

She spoke from the foot of the bed, and she was as beautiful as ever. Her hair was solidly black and arranged in a variety of buns and braids that seemed to stretch down to her waist. For every glance I stole to look directly at her, my eyes rolled back to the ceiling.

"We feed on souls," she explained. "You encounter us all the time. Usually you just feel a little tired, never quite knowing why," she spoke with a power in her voice that she never used before. "But, we are consuming you."

I gurgled again, gagging on the blood that had collected in my throat. Behind her stood a towering dark figure. Light reflected off metal rings hanging from within his robes. His face was skinless and horrible.

"No two souls are created the same," she proceeded. "But, when I met you, yours felt like one of ours." The dark figure behind her lowered himself to the foot of my bed as she continued, "And I just had to taste it to see."

My body sank into the mattress with the weight of his fists pressing down around me. Another figure approached from a crowd of others, this one floating well-above the bed and draping me within its robes of leathered skin. It's face looked to be made of worms. I winced at the sight of it.

"But it was *nothing* like ours. It was weak – vapid," she stated with contempt in her voice. "Yes, you feed off of others' souls too, but *your* soul is nothing to sustain a life," she went on. "So I had to take your body too." We made eye contact one last time, and she smiled amidst her look of disgust.

I shut my eyes as the others approached from behind her, crowding over my bed and filling the room with the smell of my death. I still knew which body was hers amongst their masses, and in anticipation of the ultimate pain and nothingness that would follow, for one more brief and wonderful moment, I swam in her waves before drowning.

VULTURES OF THE AFTERMATH

All things come in threes. The end justifies the means. The end justifies the means. The end justifies the means. Amen.

The men of my family are providers. We put food on the table – end of story. We Greberts come from a long line of 'em. More than just a satchel swinging beneath the gut, we are patriarchs. And when I moved our line, our family name came with me.

For centuries, we dug graves for the wealthy to bury their dead. Like my father before me, and his father before him, I learnt how to break ground with a shovel. But, when you shovel soil day in and day out, the body has a way of wearing down on you. Sometimes it's the shoulders, burning with each stab into that mud. Sometimes it's the back, freezing on you and making it impossible to stand upright. Sometimes it's the knees, just aching from a long day diggin'.

I had worked for a few funeral homes in my day. Sometimes shoveling, other times doing a different kind of dirty work – dressing, casketing, or cossetting the dead. We Greberts ain't just diggers, you know; we're opportunity takers. And when I seen that the real money was in owning a funeral home, I saw an opportunity, and I took it.

The job required more bookkeeping than I would have liked, but the business of caring for the dead came easy to me – being from a long line of Greberts and all. I enjoyed overseeing the process, taking a corpse to be buried and presenting it back to its fambly – using make-up and other tricks to cover up those hideous gashes and wounds that scar a body. A desairologist, they called me. A lot of it was just common sense, like tying the arms together behind the back when we presented 'em. Because, otherwise, their arms would stick up like they're reaching out to get you. Or, sometimes using some good 'ole toilet paper and glue went a long way to fill in those missing pockets of flesh – good for bullet holes and all.

While I did the meetings with fambies and the planning and decoratin' pieces of it, my boys did the diggin' for me. Had to start 'em at the bottom, teach 'em about an honest day's work and all. There was Eric. He was the oldest of the bunch and reminded me of myself – hungry to learn more, to do more. He would be first in line to take over the business after me, and he had the wit to do it too. Whatever I did, he watched and learnt – no questions asked. He was real respectful like that.

Next in line was Peter. He was named after my father, and I hoped he would be more like Eric, but he was a shy boy – gentle. I think he always wished to be in my role, meeting with the fambies, rather than getting his hands dirty in the earth. But, goddamn it, Peter, the last thing a fambly wants when they're burying their dead is to have their mortician crying like a fag in front of 'em.

Then there was Beauregard. My boy Beau. Beau was born with some kind of clinical retardation, the doctors said. Now, I never quite understood it, as he seemed to be a fine boy until one day when he wasn't. But, accordin' to them doctors, Beau was a retard. I tried to get him to do work for us. He din't listen to me much, but his brothers got him to do their work sometimes. Just a little praise and

Beau would be clapping and squealing, just pleased as can be that he made his brothers happy and all.

The business problems started early on with a big bank loan. We lived in a small town, and in a small town, people don't die all that much. So, we'd miss one payment and before you know it, one payment cost as much as three. So, if people weren't passin' away, sometimes you had to help them along. It ain't all about work ethic; I had to teach my boys about shortcuts too.

The first one I helped along was old man Mathers. Mr. Mathers had lived well into his nineties, having long survived his wife – Mrs. Mathers – and was achin' to see her. I knew Mr. Mathers well, and my boys were friends with his grandsons. So, when Mr. Mathers invited me over for a drink, I poured him a strong one, and maybe even a strong second or third. I helped him to get into bed on his back, and wouldn't you know it, he died in the middle of the night smothered in his pillow. And just like that, he saved the business! He was a bit dehydrated when I went to work on him, but some wax took care of that. His boys shook my hand and had themselves a nice little burial.

No questions were asked at the next two or three funerals, but eventually the town constable came sniffing. I welcomed him into my parlor and answered all of his questions. He *knew* the principal business strategy I employed, but with the right private donation, he pursued other leads in the mysterious accidents befalling our small town.

I encouraged a reg'lar line of business to be carted through our doors, and I enjoyed caring for those bodies. I made sure they wore their Sunday best when they returned to meet their maker – hair parted with the grain and all. Their famblies would cry when they saw how beautiful they looked. So, I never felt bad about my intention to eat well, especially after so many years of hardly eating at all. Eric had talked to me about how it was his time to takeover, that I earnt my retirement. But, I just wouldn't listen – stubborn like that, we Grebert men are.

Once the constable could no longer be encouraged, a tragedy in the shape of a swinging shovel befell the back of his head. I was surprised to learn of it myself, and I imagined my boys would be mutually pleased when they heard the news. But, when I went to tell them of it, Beau was already squealing and clapping away, proud of the work he gen'rated for the business. Before long, we were no small business, and I stood on a mound meant to be a fortune. The end justifies the means, amen.

Now, they say the last sense to go when you die is your hearing. They say the ears will keep on ringing, pickin' up on any sounds around them. I don't know that I saw any evidence of that when I was building my – let's say – clientele. I remember lookin' some of them right in the eye and thinkin' that they were long gone – far away and anywhere but here. But, for me, yessir, the hearing was the last thing to go.

The day we paid back our loan to the bank, I was gearin' up to take my boys to a steak dinner worthy of our celebration. I put on my Sunday best, and Eric saw to it that he and the boys were dressed in their finest. I was about out the door to meet the boys when I noticed a missing fire poker from the fireplace. Strange thing that a fire poker might go missing in the early evenin' on a summer day. Like a fool, I went over to it to see if it was laying nearby, and I was overwhelmed by the sound of breaking rocks. I never saw myself fall, and there was no pain – no white lights and no angels – just breaking rocks, and then a lot of squealing and happy clapping and hollerin'. Damn fools had done me in! Meant to take my fortune before I could enjoy it, not realizing they'd have to pay for my funeral – a price for which they'd have to take out another dang loan from the bank! But, just like that, my boys – like their father and his father before him – became true patriarchs and providers for their fambly. And for that, I say, "Amen."

THE WHITE CROSS ON RESSURRECTION DRIVE

There's a white cross on Resurrection Drive. Staked into the dirt about two feet off the road, it's nothing more than two wood planks nailed together and painted white – the kind of thing that already looked old the day it was made. Deteriorating through time and under the splash of mud puddles from passing cars, it will continue to age until it finally sinks into the earth many years from now. But, for right now, with bobbing green and purple balloons, it stands at the side of the road as a marker, serving its purpose while being forgotten, like a faded dollar bill.

Days ago, Mike went for a drive as he always did after leaving the local watering hole. He had the reputation of an angry young man and drove the way one would expect of him – reckless and aggressive. He knew of his reputation, but he didn't care. He just knew how he felt about certain things. If other people didn't see that the Jews owned the world and that the goddamned Mexicans and blacks were killing morality in America, then he had to make it his business to teach them. He had a bat he carried in the trunk of his car with one long railroad spike secured to it, and it was his best teaching aid. He liked to swing it and "Chase the brown out of town," as he would say.

He was a town embarrassment, especially for his politician father, who kept his own misanthropic behavior more private. But Mike never thought much of it himself – never cared. Whatever situation might arise, he had the answer on his hand: his middle finger.

For as unpredictable as Mike could be, he liked his routines and little rituals. He put his foot down the clutch of his car and turned the engine, holding on just a little bit longer than he should. After an uproar from the motor and a brief explosion of exhaust, his tires burned a black trail marking his way from the parking lot, subwoofer thumping to publicize his departure. With his skull ring and sunglasses at night, he was king and Resurrection drive was his kingdom.

Down south, places go by their local names. Back in the 1800s, the ground that constitutes RD was a burial site for the Comanche. They didn't like the idea of burying their dead at first, but the Christian missionaries were *persuasive* in their teachings. After all of the Texas-Indian wars, the land was mostly forgotten under an eventual row of cookie cutter churches – all of which have since closed, "Resurrection" being the last of them.

Local legend has it that RD's name really comes from the number of dead dogs left at the side of the road. The scavengers should have their way with the dead – the buzzards, the vultures, the insects. But that doesn't happen here. Instead, the dogs just sit there until, some time later, they're just gone. Adding to this phenomenon, a few local kids started spreading word about a drifter who was hit and left at the side of the road, saying that a week after the accident, his grave where he was buried was empty. Then again, the same kids ran into some trouble with the sheriff for dragging dog bodies from the road. But, legend still has it that the corpses just up themselves and walk away.

After making a left out of the parking lot, RD runs

straight for miles – ideal for timing a climb up and past sixty miles per hour. Mike's engine shrieked as it redlined. Picking up speed, the yellow dashed stripes on the road flew past the windows. Further down the road, he caught a stray dog in the headlights of his car. The dog, terrified, didn't budge. Mike swerved and made contact with a sickening *thump*, launching the dog from the front right corner of his already dented car. The dog made no sound – no cry – when he died. In the distance was another one. Mike's lucky night, or so he thought.

Upon hearing Mike's screeching engine, the dog started to run. Popping the clutch and shifting gears, he charged right at her, veering to the right of the road to intersect her path to the grassy brush. He followed her to the edge of the pavement but gave up once she cleared her way to safety. Soon, Mike would be nearing the end of the straight away and would turn around to do it all again. His Thursday nights ran like clockwork.

In a series of quick moves, the handbrake dragged the rear of his car into a semi-circle, tracing another set of black tire marks over his own trail from a week before. The engine yelled out in defiance when shifted into a lower gear. Usually, a series of growls would build and release from the engine as he built back his speed, but on this night, a handful of nails punctured his front right tire, forcing him to lose control of the car.

Mike threw his feet down on the clutch and brakes and ripped the wheel left and right as his semi-circle continued into full circles. His struggle to regain control of his car came to an abrupt end as the front of his car crumpled upon collision with a streetlight. His body flew into the steering wheel and collapsed back into his seat. Only then did his airbag finally release and deflate in front of him.

I stood aside the wreck from the passenger's side and watched Mike regain consciousness in the pillow of his airbag with blood dripping into his eyes from the glass that was embedded in his forehead. I watched him – dazed, bruised, and bleeding – as he leaned against the door of the car with all of his weight, his shaking hands feeling for the door handle. Once they found it, they pulled, and he fell helplessly onto the side of the road.

Pieces of gravel made their way into the open wounds of Mike's cheek with his body sprawled across the open road. The subwoofer's bass drowned his groans as he slithered forward and away from his smoking car. Meanwhile, I returned to my car parked further down the road. By the time I was back in my driver's seat, he had mustered all of his strength together to push himself onto his knees.

Mike balanced himself on all fours in the middle of the road when he saw my car slowly approaching. He lifted his head and stared blindly into the headlights. With a brain damaged look on his face, he gazed at me through the windshield in hopes to identify his savior. It was the first time I saw him with his sunglasses off; he had ugly eyes. I continued to drive towards him as he knelt humbled in the high beams of my car. I swear I saw him mouth my name. *Good. Let him know my name.* He trembled in the center of the road – blood dripping from his nose. And, as I drew closer, I watched his face grow in terror as I refused to stop.

OF GOD, MONSTERS, AND MEN

Behind a diner counter covered in old coffee stains, a small boom box played its repetitive techno hook without changing tracks or breaking for talk or commercials. It was *After Hours* on the radio waves, and it was after hours at the 24-hour pit stop – the one that seemed to have no name other than what it advertised in dying neon blue lights: "Food."

Gabe hated techno – hated it. It was the elevator music of the middle of the night as far as he was concerned. No soul, no words, just a pounding rhythm foreshadowing the booze headache to follow. Tucked away in a booth near the center of the diner, he stacked coffee creamers while he waited for his date to arrive. He thought about potential points of conversation now that they had left the bar and were without their group of mutual friends, but he found himself distracted by his elbows becoming wet from the recently cleaned table.

"Hey," Andrea said. She snuck up on him, causing him to jump and tip his coffee creamer tower over. "Oops, didn't mean to topple your tower," she said with a full smile. "Turns out, you got me pretty liquored up."

"OK, well here, let's get a head start on fighting that

hangover then," Gabe replied. He handed her a menu.

Andrea flashed a brief and polite smile. "Well, listen, Gabe, I was actually thinking that maybe I should just go home. It's late, and I'm not feeling that great."

"No, no, c'mon," Gabe pleaded with his own polite smile – more forced than Andrea's forfeit expression. "We were having a nice night. We got a few drinks in us, some good conversation," he suggested.

Andrea looked down for a second, seeming to think about it.

"And we just got here," Gabe added.

"You're right," Andrea replied after another pause. "And we're celebrating tonight," she said.

"Oh yeah?" Gabe replied with surprise.

Andrea glanced at him with silence. "Last weekend I did something *bad*, and tonight is the one week-a-versary," she clarified.

"I don't want to jinx myself, but I like the sound of that," Gabe joked. "I'll cheers to being another one of your bad decisions." He smiled and held up his glass of water before taking a sip.

"Believe me, Gabe, *no* decisions have been made here about *you* tonight," she stated with raised eyebrows and a hint of contempt in her voice.

"All right, well, I don't know that I really want to hear about your bad decision from last week," Gabe replied.

"No, it wasn't like that. Last weekend was a good decision to do something bad," she clarified further.

Gabe waited before responding, "All right, I'll bite. What did you do that was so bad?" he asked.

"It's a secret." Andrea winked and hid herself behind a sip of water from her glass. She held the power in this conversation and reveled in it.

"I see…" Gabe said. "So, how *bad* are we talking?"

"*Real bad*, Gabe. But, good, too," she paused. "I introduced some justice into the world."

"Justice, huh? Are you about to reveal your secret

superhero identity to me?" Gabe asked.

"You wish." Andrea took another sip of her water, her contempt becoming less disguised. "Let me ask you this, Gabe, do you believe in fate?"

"Do I believe in fate?" he repeated the question to himself. "Absolutely."

"So you don't believe in chance or freewill, then?" she asked.

Gabe paused to think for a second before responding, "No. I believe in destiny – like things are destined to happen." Gabe leaned over to his right with continued thought, "You don't?"

"No. I think we all have freewill – no fate, no destiny." She waited before continuing and lost her smile in the process, "No rule or order to life – just randomness and chaos."

An air of silence fell between them and Andrea noticed the techno that had been pumping from the small stereo behind the counter for the first time.

"Ed-juh-muh-cate me," Gabe smiled.

"You're still drunk," Andrea jabbed.

"I sure hope so!" Gabe quipped. "I was hoping you were too!"

"Oh, I'm feeling it," she replied. "I don't usually drink like that, but I needed it tonight."

"Oh yeah, how's that?" Gabe asked.

Andrea flashed that quick smile of hers – a smile that awarded her more tips than she earned as a waitress, rounded her B grades to A's, and crippled ex-boyfriends with insecurity when she aimed it elsewhere.

"C'mon now, needed a drink to have fun with 'ole Gabe here?" he asked with more sincerity than he meant to reveal. He raised his eyes to meet hers.

Andrea remained silent.

Gabe picked up a packet of fake sugar and twirled it between his fingers before standing it upright on the table with his left hand and flicking it with his right. It soared through the air and landed square in her water. *Hole in one!*

"Real mature," Andrea jabbed again. "You're right, we're still on our date." Andrea dragged out the last of her words, mocking him, "So let's have fun."

"Tell me about your chaos, pretty lady," Gabe invited. Their lack of chemistry did not register to him.

"You said you believe that there is some form of law and order in the universe. So, you also believe in karma then, right? Like Fascist Mike getting run over on the very street where he liked to hit dogs," Andrea paused with brief concern that *she* shouldn't be the one to talk about the irony of what happened to Mike. Maybe she was more liquored up than she thought.

"Uh huh," Gabe followed.

"So, if you do something, then you have a consequence coming to you. Reap what you sew, right?" Andrea continued, nodding for emphasis. "See, I think the world is a big sandbox for us to play in. And, if you do something good or bad, it makes no difference. But, it would be nice if it did – if there were justice in the world," she paused again to see if Gabe was still following her. "The only karma that exists is in the consequences we create ourselves. So it's up to us."

Gabe listened quietly before responding with disinterest, "Yeah, I dig it." He waved his hand over to the waitress behind the counter. A petite young woman in a yellow uniform made her way over to their table. "Hang on," Gabe said to Andrea.

"Ya'all ready to order?" the waitress asked.

"Yeah, bacon," Gabe said.

"Two orders?" she asked.

"Yes," Gabe replied with confidence. He looked to Andrea for confirmation. She nodded.

"Anything else?" the waitress asked. Gabe looked to Andrea, who shook her head in response.

"No," he hesitated. "Wait, yeah."

"What's that, hon?" she asked.

"We're taking a poll," he said.

"Shut up," Andrea whispered under her breath. She dropped her head onto her hands, hiding her face.

"Life… is it total chaos or is there a reason things happen?" Gabe asked.

"I don't know, hon. God is good enough for me. I've got to get back to these other gentlemen's tables," the waitress answered.

Other gentlemen? Gabe looked around the room. There was one cook and two patrons. The cook – a balding middle-aged man covered in grease stains – was back in the kitchen. Tucked way on the other side of the diner was a trucker in red flannel with blue suspenders. Near him, a businessman in a beige trench coat sat over an early breakfast or a late night snack, depending on how you wanted to look at it. *That's a late night snack to me*, Gabe thought.

"So, freewill and fate," Andrea continued, "God is another option. You can believe or not believe in randomness and believe or not believe in God," she explained. "It gets complicated."

"You know how I know the universe isn't random?" Gabe asked. "Because I've got bad luck," Gabe said. "Bad luck, like, consistently."

Andrea leaned in. "Maybe that's because you make bad choices, Gabe," she said without a smile to hide her distaste for him.

"I'll prove it. Watch this," Gabe said. He took a coin out of his pocket. "If I flip this coin ten times, I should be able to guess it right half the time. Right? It should be fifty-fifty odds. But, watch, I'll guess it wrong every single time."

Andrea scoffed. "You can guess ten coin flips wrong? Why is that impressive?"

"That's still more than chance. It's hard to be one hundred percent wrong the same way it's hard to be one hundred percent right," Gabe explained.

"OK," Andrea quipped. "Show me."

Gabe flipped the coin. "Heads!" he exclaimed. He turned it over to show that it came up tails. He flipped again and shouted, "Heads!" The coin came up tails.

"OK, zero for two so far," Andrea said.

Gabe flipped the coin again. "Tails!" he yelled. It was heads. He smiled at her with growing confidence and flipped it again. He yelled, "Heads!" and it came up tails. But, his luck ended there. His next six coin flips came up exactly as he called them.

"Ok, let me get this straight. You flipped a coin ten times and got it wrong four out of ten times. How isn't that chance?" Andrea asked.

Gabe looked down deflated. "That's never happened before," he said.

"Well, I guess you were right!" Andrea exclaimed. "You were wrong about guessing incorrectly, which continues your streak of being wrong. Or, in this case, you continued a streak of bad choices by making a bad bet." Andrea smiled with authentic enthusiasm for the second time on the night. "It's all random!" she continued. "I've known people – good people – who get hurt when they don't deserve it! And, I've known bad people who don't get hurt at all," she said with anger. "There is *no* rhyme or reason for any of it. None unless you *make some*." She wiped a mental image of Fascist Mike from her mind's eye and put her hands flat on the table, considering again whether or not it was time for her to go home.

Gabe fell quiet, and the techno from the radio counted their beats of silence. "There was this game we used to play as kids," he started. His voice was softer; the excitement from the night had left him. "We called it, 'God, Monsters, and Men,' and we would play it with a deck of cards. It was kind of like rock-paper-scissors in a way, but with slapping. There would be six of us neighborhood kids who would play. And what we would do is take the kings, jacks, and one ace out of a deck of cards, shuffle 'em up, and then deal them. The dealer was God, because he would get to choose what everyone else's card was and would sit out to watch the game. Then the rest of us would run around and trade cards. If you had a king or a jack, you were a man. But if you had the ace, then you were a monster. If you were a king and you found out who the jacks were, you would get to slap that kid across the face real hard. And if you were a monster, you could slap whoever carried a jack or a king. And the jacks, they just tried to lie about what card they had so that they could finish the game without getting slapped. Sometimes there were more jacks or more kings, and the game ended once everyone knew what card everyone else had. It was kind of rigged against the jacks."

Andrea listened and waited for more.

"I got a lot of bloody noses playing that game," Gabe confessed with a short smirk, hoping to create a punch line to his story. His eyes focused on the table.

"So?" Andrea asked.

"I always had a jack," Gabe explained.

"So you were bad at picking cards – self-fulfilling prophecy," she suggested.

"No, I mean, I was *always*, a jack. The game was fixed, Andrea. Whoever got to be God and picked the other cards, they would always make me a jack and cheated so that everyone else always had an ace. There were no other jacks or kings when I played," he went on with exasperation that she missed the point. "A lot of bloody noses," he said louder than before.

"So why did you keep playing it?" Andrea asked.

"It was the only way they would let me play with them," Gabe said, his gaze returned to the table.

The somber tone of the evening had finally settled upon them. Andrea reached her hand over to Gabe. He reached forward to meet her and placed his hands in hers. Andrea smiled with wide eyes (*real smile number three*, Gabe noted). "That's not luck, Gabe, that's just being kind of dumb!" Andrea pulled her hands back and leaned away with laughter.

"Bacon's here," the waitress chimed in and placed two plates on the table.

"Oh, that smells good!" Andrea exclaimed. "Good idea on this, Gabe," she said with her smile still on her face.

"Yeah," Gabe muttered under his breath.

Following Gabe's deflation, the power cut out. It was a dark night, but the large lamps in the parking lot cast enough light into the small diner to see everyone's disconcerted reaction. They all picked up their heads as if they were waiting for a notification that everything was all right.

"Not to worry, prob'ly just a fuse. Air conditioning likes to throw a hissy fit sometimes," the cook called out. "I'll go check on it in a second."

In the semi-dark, the waitress walked over to Gabe and Andrea's booth. "Can I get ya'll anything else?" she asked. She had blond curls and was pretty despite her crooked teeth. 'Stacey,' her nametag read.

"No, I think we've about had it," Gabe said. "If we could just get the check, please." He hated that techno, but he was unsettled sitting in the dark without it.

"Jesus jumpin' Christ!" the trucker yelled with spit flying from his lips. Gabe jumped at the exclamation, whirling his head around but not knowing what he was looking for. Andrea's eyes followed.

The trucker brought his napkin to his lips with one hand and pointed to a silhouette outside carrying a bat with a spike. The figure raised the bat and brought it down on the windshield of Andrea's car.

"Bob!" Stacey called. But, Bob – the cook – had already left to go find the fuse.

"Look at this summuh-muh bitch!" the trucker exclaimed. He struggled to get out of the booth, catching his stomach on the underside of the table.

"The fuck–" Gabe was cut off by Andrea screaming.

Her eyes caught the figure in black, from his boots to his misshapen head. He continued to bring the bat down the headlights of her car.

"What in the hell?" the businessman chimed in.

"Bob!" Stacey continued to call out. Still no reply.

"Call the cops!" the businessman commanded.

"Isn't that your car?" Gabe asked Andrea in disbelief. He turned back to Andrea who looked as if she was on the edge of fainting. "Andrea!"

Her eyes rolled up and closed as she fell back into the booth. Gabe continued to try to grasp the situation but couldn't. Was he supposed to go to Andrea or supposed to fight this thing away from her car?

"The line's dead," Stacey reported as she slammed the down the phone. She went back to calling Bob's name. Bob remained silent.

"Well, c'mon. I got a shotgun in my cab," the trucker suggested.

"I wouldn't go out there," the businessman replied as he joined the small group huddling around Andrea and Gabe's booth at the center of the small diner. Meanwhile, the figure outside proceeded to move from the headlights to the windows of Andrea's car. They shattered with greater ease than Gabe would have imagined.

After finishing the windows, the figure turned towards the group of them, revealing his twisted face. It looked as if it had been crushed in a vice, *or maybe under the treads of a car tire*, Gabe thought.

The sight of the disfigured man sucked the wind from the trucker's lungs. The businessman moved over to the front door, and Gabe followed with a feeling of lightness. His adrenaline was pumping, but he wouldn't dare bring himself to go outside unarmed. He considered grabbing a kitchen knife, *but you don't bring a knife to a spiked-bat fight*, he thought.

"There are hardly any cops on this route at this hour. We've got to do something," the trucker proposed.

"Seems like he's really got something against that car. Maybe he'll go away when he's done," the businessman suggested. He turned to Gabe, "Don't worry son. I know a great lawyer." He raised his hand to point to Andrea. "She won't pay a dime." Meanwhile, Andrea was sound asleep in her booth.

"Ohmygodohmygod!" Stacey called out. The three men turned to find Stacey stepping back from the door to the kitchen with her hands over her mouth. The businessman made his way over and pulled at the door to the kitchen, revealing Bob's body lying at the opposite side of the door. A gaping hole was planted in his forehead; a single line of red ran from the wound down the side of his face and into a puddle beneath his head.

The trucker turned to Gabe, "Let's go get that shotgun, son, and put an end to this." Before they could turn to make their way towards the parking lot, the front door shattered, sending a blast of bladed glass into their backs. The man-thing stood like a statue with his weapon by his side.

The trucker turned towards the figure and rushed at him, carrying his four hundred plus pounds like a linebacker. The figure raised his bat over his shoulder and walked towards the charging trucker, meeting him halfway. In a single motion, he swung the bat with one hand, driving its spike into the trucker's neck and sending him to the ground. The trucker's fall rattled the tables in the diner. He let out a groan, pained more by the fall than the punctured hole in his neck. Blood poured from him, his body's movements slowing until finally stopping.

Stacey stood frozen with the businessman by the door to the kitchen, both of them horrified by the murder scene unfolding before them. The figure continued towards them, revealing his half-destroyed face covered in a mixture of blood and mud. It was difficult to tell if pieces of his skull and face were missing or if they had been crushed together. Gabe took to shaking Stacey by the shoulders, snapping her to attention. "Is there a back exit? Is there another exit?" he yelled.

The businessman let out a shriek, as if his voice were an audio recording suddenly taken off pause.

"Shut up! Get a hold of yourself!" Gabe commanded to the businessman over his shoulder.

Stacey stared back at Gabe blankly.

"Is there another exit?" Gabe repeated.

The businessman stepped sideways towards the door with his hands raised, meeting the monster eye to eye. "Listen, I'm a very rich man. I can give you whatever you want. Just tell me what you want," he said. His voice was nervous and unsure.

The monster appeared to listen, despite the pieces of brain that hung out from the side of his head. While one side of his face remained emotionless, the other half – the dead half – began to turn to a frown.

"I can give you what you want. Just tell me," the businessman pleaded.

"He's dead. Look at him!" Stacey yelled.

"He's not acting dead," Gabe added.

"Whatever you want! What is it?" the businessman bargained with desperation in his voice.

The half-faced man tilted his head and pointed towards Andrea, his dead stare gazing past the businessman.

"Her?" the businessman asked. "You want her?"

Gabe had been watching the scene unfold from over his shoulder as he pushed at the door with Stacey. "No one's going to get her," Gabe called back with pressured words – more to the businessman than to the monster.

"Here – go on and take her," the businessman offered as he motioned towards Andrea, who was unaware of the horror show happening around her. The half-faced man turned his glance back towards the businessman, his bat raised high. "Just take her!" the businessman offered one last time before the half-faced man slammed his bat down and split the businessman's skull like rotted wood.

Stacey screamed again, gathering the thing's attention. She charged her shoulder into the kitchen door, failing to move it and also dropping a key ring from her hand and into Bob's blood puddle that had gathered at her feet. The man-thing approached them as they scrambled to gain their footing in Bob's spilled blood.

Rather than bending down to reach for the keys, Stacey took a knife from the diner's counter and ran at the half-faced man. Her blade found his gut, and Gabe saw the thing bleed, but he also saw that his guts were mostly missing, as if they had already fallen out of him.

With Stacey pressed in close to him, the thing took his available hand and placed it over Stacey's face, with the skull ring from his finger cutting into her skin. He squeezed, snaring her in his grasp. His hand muffled her screams as he closed his grip on her face and fractured her delicate bones. In time, her shrieking sounds withered into silence.

Gabe grabbed for the wet key ring, frustrated by his hand's shakiness. He pushed the door against Bob's body, finally clearing enough room to make his way into the kitchen. As he struggled with the door, Andrea awoke and screamed from the booth, drawing the man-thing's attention towards her. Under his gaze, she got to her feet and ran to Gabe.

"C'mon!" Gabe yelled to Andrea from the door to the kitchen. He clutched the keys in his hands and hoped there would be an exit in the back. The half-faced man watched Andrea sprint for the kitchen. Once she made it through, she and Gabe kicked Bob's body back into place, blocking the door.

"There has to be a way out back here!" Gabe yelled at Andrea. They moved past an industrial table and freezer in the dark.

"Here!" Andrea pointed to the outline of a door, etched by lighting from outside. Behind them, the bat struck at the kitchen door, knocking a hole into it. Andrea tried the door handle at the back exit but it was locked.

"I got it," Gabe took the first key from the key ring and tried to match it to the door's lock. He couldn't tell if it didn't fit or if his nervous hands were just making it impossible to use. He scrambled for the next one, which also didn't fit. Another bat swing tore the kitchen door behind them in half.

"C'mon Gabe!" Andrea screamed at him.

"I'm trying!" he attempted the third key on the ring, which also didn't fit. Another kick at the door shattered it, and the man-thing stepped over Bob's dead body into the kitchen.

"C'mon you bastard!" Gabe exclaimed, fumbling with the keys again. He was onto the fourth of the six keys – still no match. The man-thing continued to approach them, dragging his bat on the ground behind him.

In frustration, Gabe jammed the fifth key into the key hole, but it wouldn't budge left or right. "Here, it has to be this one!" Gabe handed the sixth and final key to Andrea.

"Gabe, no!" she yelled, crying as he left her at the locked door and met the man-thing just an arm's reach away.

As Gabe met him face-to-face, his gut swirled with nausea. The thing snarled at him, his week-dead breath hanging in the air. The man-thing raised an arm and pushed Gabe, forcing him to the ground. Gabe crab-walked backwards until he was pressed against the freezer.

Andrea screamed and sobbed as she stood at the locked door, doing her best to push the sixth and final key into the keyhole. It would fit; it *had* to fit! If there truly were any order to the universe, someone or something would save her and Gabe. Her cries said that she was ready to believe that – ready to believe in anything but randomness. After all, what did Gabe do to deserve this?

From behind her, Andrea heard Gabe plead, "Please, please don't." He had calm in his voice. He had given up. And, just like the countless times he drew a jack before, he was a second late to raise his hands in defense when the slap came. Though, this slap was with the blunt side of a spiked bat, and it took the teeth from his mouth, the vision from his eyes, and the life from his body.

Andrea's final key did not fit. She rapped at the door with her first, her face pressed against it, screaming and crying for help as the sound of the awful bat dragged its way towards her. "Please. Somebody!" she begged through choked tears before her head was broken and smeared against the locked door.

EMPLOYEE ASSISTANCE PROGRAM

Entry 1

09/07/14

Well, well, well, here we are again, Blinking Curser Friend – always tapping your foot and waiting with impatience for the next line of text to be typed. I'm starting to remember why I gave you up; we never satisfy one another – you and I. Ha! And just like that, I've broken the essential rule of Creative Writing 101: no writing about writing.

So, here we are bumping into one another in the middle of the night like strangers. I've put on a few pounds and lost some hair since the last time we met. I hope you recognize me. But you look the same; the years have been good to you. I really didn't want to meet you like this, but I guess I was *encouraged* to reach out to you again. And, if we're going to keep meeting like this with any kind of regularity, I think it's important that we start on the right foot. So, in the spirit of honesty, let's put it all out there. Let me tell you why I'm coming to you like this.

About a week ago, I was told that I had a bit of a "meltdown" at work. Is there any validity to that complaint? Absolutely not. I was there, and there was no meltdown. Nonetheless, I was told that if I wanted to keep my job, it was *suggested* that I start going to therapy. It's like playing a game of Monopoly and drawing the "Go to Jail for Fifty Minutes a Week for Six Weeks" card.

Anyway, I met with the therapist last week. She's a nice woman – a bit young, maybe – but she seemed competent and capable. We talked about "anger management" and different times in my life where I have been in trouble due to anger. And then we talked about other times in my life where I've not been angry. That's where you come in, Blinking Curser. She explained that when we were together, I had an "outlet" for my "feelings." Some doctors prescribe medicine, but this one prescribed writing in a journal at least once a week. OK.

I told her I needed a prompt, but she said just write about anything. Even about writing? *Even about writing.* Session 1 done. Entry 1 done.

Entry 2

09/08/14

Today, we talked about what happened that led up to the "meltdown" at work. I insisted there was no "meltdown." She told me about this idea of "congruence," that that's where the "meltdowns" come from. She said that if I am not congruent with myself, then that feels bad. But, it's hard to live your life feeling bad, and so the *role* of my meltdowns (anger) is to take action in my life to make changes to increase congruence. She says that whether I am aware of it or not, that's what I'm trying to do.

I explained to *her* that if you take a person who is sane and rational and competent and capable and then drop him off into a world where everyone around him is insane, irrational, incompetent, and incapable, then the *sane* person will appear *insane* because what constitutes normal is all relative to the majority. I think I made my point, because all she could say was that no one was suggesting that I was insane.

Entry 3

09/15/14

I learned a new vocabulary word today: trigger. A "trigger" is a thing that happens that "sets off" the "meltdowns." So, she wanted to know what happened the day that I got in trouble for the "meltdown." I reminded her that it was the idiot in the cubicle across from me having the meltdown. I do not melt, and, even if I did, it would not be in a downward way. No meltdowns.

Thinking about that day, I ended up telling her about Mary Anne and her formal complaint against me. Apparently, she went to the boss explaining that I made her feel "unsafe." *Unsafe?* Between you and me, Blinking Curser, I think it's just easier for the company to refer me to an EAP for anger management than to deal with the dysfunction that is Mary Anne.

Have you ever seen someone with a punchable face? That's her. It's the kind of face, that when you see it, it looks like it needs to be slapped real hard. You know the kind – eyes that stare off into space, not really focused on anything, a mouth that hangs open a little bit, caught in a perpetual, "Uhhhhhhh?" That about sums her up. It's not so much my opinion as just a matter of fact.

Entry 4

09/23/14

Here we are four weeks in, and finally there is something I can get behind: *positive visualization.* The Doc wants me to close my eyes, take some deep breaths, and picture myself having the kind of life I want to have. Finally, something to *do.*

This morning, I was stuck in traffic on the way to work and gave it a try. I closed my eyes, felt my hands gripping the steering wheel, and I imagined bumping into Mary Anne later at lunch. In this visualization, we both went to the same place to eat and ran into one another just a block or so from the restaurant. Being polite, I shook her hand, even though it was a little limp and clammy. She had to use hand sanitizer immediately afterwards just for making contact with me. Then, we talked about how nice it was to see each other, and I suggested that we ought to catch up. I led her down an alley right there, telling her I knew a shortcut to an even better place where we could get a drink. Once we were in the alley, I grabbed a broken bottle laying on the ground and jammed it into her back. *Zen.* Turned it like a corkscrew into her spine. *Zen master.*

Entry 5

09/25/14

I'm not the only one with a problem with Mary Anne. She just sued another coworker because his dog "bit" her fingers. I saw her hand, and it was fine – no blood, no cuts, no guts, no glory. But, because his dog is a pit bull, it looks bad in the eyes of the court, and he has to be "put to sleep." I'll tell you who needs to be put to sleep.

Today's visualization featured Mary Anne and I as the last workers in the office at night. In this episode, she was struggling to use the copier because she's too stupid to figure out how to operate it, and I went over and showed her that she had to place her head on the glass first. Once her face was pressed against the glass, I took the lid of the thing and slammed it over her head. It wasn't enough to kill her, and it didn't even really hurt her that bad, but oh boy, did it feel good.

Entry 6

09/29/14

Let me state some facts to you: (1) I went to get a coffee out of the shared kitchen at the office, (2) Mary Anne was standing alone in the kitchen before I arrived, (3) I turned to leave the kitchen without interacting with Mary Anne. Those are the facts. An objective observer would have to acknowledge and agree with those three points. Yet, later, I heard Mary Anne gossiping with another coworker about how I am passive-aggressively avoiding her and creating a "hostile work environment." Sure enough, another formal complaint got sent down the line, and I am now on my final "meltdown" warning before I get fired. Wow, un-believable how much power this woman wields.

Let me tell you about the worst part about interacting with Mary Anne – directly or indirectly. It's hearing her talk. She does this giggle and chuckle thing that interrupts her speech – a guckle, if you will. Unwittingly, she draws people in to listen harder and for longer, because if you don't lean in, you'll lose her words and the story, which typically lacks a purposeful end anyway. I say "unwittingly" because this woman is incapable of wit.

Anyway, the feedback that Doc keeps giving me is to watch my "triggers" and how I "cope" with them in order to avoid a "meltdown." Again, there was no meltdown; there never was. This time, I was caught in a double bind where I was damned if I did (enter the kitchen) and damned if I didn't (avoid the kitchen), to which the Doc asked me, "Where else in your life do you feel like you're damned if you do and damned if you don't?" How about right here, Doc?

Today's visualization took place after I overheard Mary Anne's gossip. We were standing in the office kitchen when I imagined taking the coffee from Mary Anne's mug and poured it down her back. She shrieked and hollered. Oh yes. Then, I took her head and held it in the kitchen sink as it filled up with water.

The last visualization got me through the workday, but when I got home, I needed another one – a nightcap, so to speak – to fall asleep. In this one, I grabbed her by the hair and dragged her into the elevator at the office, across the rooftop, and then kicked her over the side of the building. But, as she fell over the ledge and to the street below, she was giggling and chuckling (guckling) because she knew I would get caught and spend the rest of my life in prison. To her, it would be worth it to be sacrificed and victimized, so long as she knew it would ruin me too. There she was falling ass-backwards down to her death, smiling and laughing at me the whole way down. I don't think she ever hit the ground in that one.

Obviously, I couldn't sleep after that, so I did a third visualization to cope with the failure of the second one. I showed up to Mary Anne's apartment with a cake telling her that I wanted to apologize for all of the work-related drama. We sat down to have the cake together, and when I saw that she had eaten her slice of it, I revealed to her that it was made with rat poison! I sat at her kitchen table across from her laughing. The thing is, as I kept visualizing this last part, she didn't die in this one either. She just sat there, like she was waiting for a train or a bus to come for her. But, when death never arrived for her, she started laughing too. Before I knew it, the visualization was of her laughing at me while I sat at her kitchen table waiting for the police to arrive.

Entry 7

10/10/14

Dear Blinking Curser Friend,

Things have escalated. About a week ago, I went to the boss to make an informal complaint against Mary Anne, suggesting that her complaints ought to be verified or cross-checked with other sources. The boss totally agreed with that idea. But, before anything could be done, Mary Anne submitted a final complaint against me, which ultimately led to me getting fired. She stated that I was sexually harassing her by staring at her. But, believe me, if you ever saw her, you would know that no one would look at her and have any kind of a sexual thought.

With that, I was dismissed and let go from my job. The worst part about it was how sad everyone was to see me go. The boss told me that her hands were tied and, regrettably, there was nothing that could be done. Though, she also said she would do whatever she could to serve as a reference to help me land my next job.

When I was first fired, I was in such a funk that I missed my last appointment with the Doc and had to reschedule for tomorrow.

But wait! Cheer up! This story ends with good news; I promise. So, how did we turn this frown upside down? I'm glad you asked. Well, as you know, the Doc had been talking a lot about meltdowns, and I've always insisted that I hadn't had any. But, this idea about "congruence" was hanging around in the back of my mind, and I really started to give it some thought. If I want to start living the life I want to have for myself, I have to take some action, right? So, the day after I was fired, I had a meltdown – a fully sanctioned and intentional one.

A few days after I went home with all of my things, I went back to the office parking garage in the midafternoon and waited around for Mary Anne after her workday ended. Taking more breaks than anybody else throughout her day, she doesn't get much accomplished, and she is typically the last to leave the office (over-time bonus! Ka-ching). The idiot that she is, she also doesn't lock her car, assuming that security cameras in the parking garage deter any trouble. Of course, she doesn't know how to differentiate a security camera from a decoy camera with a blinking light. So, all of this is to say that I helped myself to the backseat of her car where I practiced a variety of positive visualizations over the course of the day while I waited for her. There was one involving a knife, another involving rope, and another four or five featuring various farming tools. But, those visualizations are beside the point. Once she finally came to her car and drove away from the parking garage, I sat up from the backseat – surprising the shit out of her – placed my hands on her chin and forehead, and twisted. There was a loud and forceful snap that was as gratifying in sound as it was to create. Her car veered off to the side of the road and decelerated until it ran into a tree. Admittedly, in all of my practiced visualizations, I never thought to visualize how to stop her car after snapping her neck. That's OK, I escaped with only scrapes and bruises!

But, here's where the rubber really meets the road. With my recent firing and with Mary Anne deceased in a car accident ("Oh, she was so tired from all the hours she was putting in at work that she fell asleep behind the wheel and crashed her car and snapped her friggin' neck – oh boo-hoo!"), the company needed to fill two vacant positions. So, to solve their problem, they created a new position. I applied for the job, and with my previous experience and my boss's support (and without Mary Anne there to complain), I was hired for the position along with a huge salary increase! So, tomorrow, I will officially start my new job and say goodbye to the Doc. It turns out she was right all along; you really do just have to visualize the life you want to have. After our work together, I can truly say that I feel better now than I have in longer than I can remember.

THINGS IN THE ATTIC

She pulled the ladder down from the ceiling, cringing as it groaned in protest. The general rule for sneaking into the attic in the middle of the night was to be as quiet as possible, but she wasn't practiced at it, and the ladder wasn't aligned with her mission. No matter – her parents were pretty sound sleepers and generally preoccupied anyway. She pumped her foot on the bottom step to make sure it would hold her weight. Once she felt it was secure, she placed a flashlight in her mouth and shimmied her way into the ceiling, shuffling across patches of insulation and strategically placed floorboards, stray nails, cobwebs, and things that crawl. God, how she hated that attic.

The storm had woken her – a large blast of thunder that shook the whole house – but it was her grief that kept her awake. Something strange happens when death takes up residence in your home; the atmosphere somehow becomes thicker – heavier – and everyday movements feel like you're doing them through water. Even mundane chores like taking out the garbage require a new level of effort. She was learning about the strangeness of it all, like how she could be exhausted and wide awake at the same time. Maybe that's what death does; it forces some kind of juxtaposition of contrasting things: all of your greens are framed by reds, you're hungry but you don't want to eat, and you're alive but you wish you were dead.

She swung her flashlight in an arc to clear away spider webs. In the middle of the night, the sounds of the house were more pronounced, and even more so from the silent attic – the hollow plunk of rain hitting gutters, the whirring start of the sump pump kicking in. It felt like a lifetime had passed since she was a girl scout, but, even so, she counted the seconds between flashes of lightning and clashes of thunder. What was the point of that anyway? It was clear the storm was on top of the house and not happening miles away.

Her beam stopped on half-torn boxes, plastic bins, and large shapes covered in protective cloths. Flares of lightning lit the attic in wholesale flashes. As a little girl, she would have been frightened by what could have been hiding under the cloths or behind the boxes – by what might be watching her from the darkest corners of the room.

Another crash of thunder rattled the things in the attic and shook the floorboards under her slipper-covered feet. She moved the beam from one cloth-covered mountain shape to the next. Her parents had a tendency to hold onto things long past their due. *We bury our people in the ground and their things in the attic in this family,* she thought. She made her way past tall vertical stacks of newspapers and magazines and found the specific cloth-covered mountain she was looking for.

She hunched over to avoid the beams in the ceiling and waddled towards a tall, thin shape covered by a white sheet. It was easy to spot not because of its size and figure but because the white sheet was the cleanest in the attic – not yet aged or concealed by dust or cobwebs; her light appeared to bounce off of it when she found it. As she approached it and raised her hand to reach for it, she considered her horror if a hand were to reach back at her.

She scoffed at the idea but shrank back with the slamming of another sharp crash of thunder.

"Oh my God, Ash, get it together," she whispered to herself. She reached back for the cloth and tore it away in one motion, revealing her grandmother's antique cheval mirror. It looked just as she remembered it – standing tall and proud with its clouded glass mirror plate secured in its mahogany frame. Looking into it now, she could have just as well been a little girl again wearing her grandmother's rose-colored shoes and pink scarves. A smile formed with the memory and began to quiver. Tears formed in the corners of her eyes and her throat swelled with sadness at the realization that her grandmother no longer and never again would stand behind her in its reflection. She knew that, but somehow seeing her solitary figure gave her a felt sense of that loss – something that she would later struggle to find the words to express to her friend Val. She would have begun to sob if not for becoming distracted by seeing herself cry in the reflection of the mirror. The loss of her grandmother was her first real confrontation with death, and it became something she had to wrestle with – negotiating how much she allowed herself to experience her own sense of mourning and how much she allowed others to see her grief.

She wiped at her eyes with her wrists, noting that her hands were covered in dirt and grime. Rain continued to rail at the roof above her, and somehow in this moment, she felt all right. She uncovered another one of death's strange juxtapositions; the most normal she felt in the three days following her grandmother's death came during a thunderstorm in the middle of the night as she sat on a cracked plywood board in the attic by her grandmother's old mirror. The realization reminded her of something she had just read on a message board for New Agers. Someone had posted something along the lines of saying that with all forms of art, we try to create externally what we feel internally. As a little girl, she was forced into piano

103

lessons by her mom, and she approached the instrument with the same excitement she had when she was given a bag of socks on her ninth birthday. "Well, you need them," her mom had assured her. What she really wanted was to play guitar in a punk band. But her mom had a way of silencing those aspirations with her scoffs, eye rolls, and the scripted, "Ashley, please." So, maybe her real calling was in performance art. She made sure to make a mental note of that as a point of discussion for drama class.

Alas, she found what she was looking for – an item connected to the person she lost, which also happened to be a mirror (the second thing she needed), and a quiet space to try to contact the dead undisrupted. She sat down with her legs folded and placed herself in front of the mirror with the flashlight shining upwards from the ground. In that position, she could see her face reflected in the mirror and not much else. Following the instructions from the website, she began the process with an invitation for spirits to reveal themselves to her.

She rested her hands in her lap and allowed herself to relax. With her eyes closed, she took a deep breath and stated her intention, "I am here to speak with my grandmother. I will only receive messages from her. I will not see, hear, or acknowledge any other spirits." With her intention stated, she opened her eyes and gazed upon her reflection in the mirror.

A few people who posted on the site said it took somewhere between two and five minutes to work. It wasn't a complicated process, just one you had to be open for. "If you don't believe it will work, it won't," she was cautioned. Well, she was ready to believe. She was well aware that she wished to speak to her grandmother to tell her for at least one definite last time that she loved her and missed her. There wasn't much else to say anyway. Her grandmother had been old and sick and getting sicker. There was no surprise in her death, and Ashley's sadness wasn't for her grandmother; it was for herself – for missing the one person in the world she felt she could count on above and beyond anyone else. But, more profoundly, if this mirror experiment worked – if she really could see or contact the dead – then that would prove that there was more to this life after all. Her parents made her attend church more than she would have liked, and she excelled in bible school, but the habit of attendance could not force a sense of belief for her. Her parents were some of the most religious people she had ever met. And, yet, they were also some of the unhappiest people she knew. So, either this religion thing was nonsense and just another way for her parents to try to control her in order to ease their own anxiety about raising a strong young woman in a dangerous world, or her parents were morons. Sometimes, she suspected both things were true.

At first glance, her face reflected back to her and looked like her own. Her sleek jawline was highlighted in the beam of her flashlight, her cheekbones accentuated by shadows, and her eyes made even more dark and piercing. She noticed the smooth skin that ran across her forehead, no longer riddled with traces of acne now that summer had ended and she no longer wore a headband to play tennis. If it were up to her, she would have played lacrosse instead, but that was "unladylike," and so it was a summer of tennis and headbands and acne.

It had been a while, she realized, since she just looked at herself in the mirror without a purpose, just noticing her face and herself without mindfully picking apart everything that she wished looked different. She imagined how much her face had changed since she was a child, back when she used to wish that she could imagine what she would look like as an adult or as an elderly woman – like her grandmother, perhaps.

It was in the midst of that thought that her reflection began to change, softening in some places, rounding in others, as if someone had placed a squirming mask over her. She started to gasp as her face evolved in front of her, but she paused her reaction to not interrupt the process.

Steadily, her face began to transform into others' faces. She would appear older and more mature only to devolve and reform to a more youthful face the next second. She watched in amazement as her contours grew and shrank. It was real, and it was happening, and she gazed on with eager anticipation for her grandmother's face to appear before her.

As the cycle of changing faces cascaded over her own, one face appeared for a second time and lingered. It was the face of an old woman – darker and more haggard than any woman she had ever known. Whereas the other faces appeared as masks spawned from her own image, this face appeared to exist in its own right and stared back at her, threatening her before dissolving into the next face, one of a woman in her twenties.

Quickly, the young woman rotated and aged to a middle-aged woman. Just as quickly as Ashley noticed the seriousness of her expression, she melted into a youthful child. The stream of faces continued to transform over her own, and Ashley found herself imagining what her life would be like if the faces she saw were, indeed, her own. She watched in bewilderment as the lines in her forehead deepened and softened, as her cheeks rose and descended, until the haggard woman's face returned once more. Again, the old woman stared back at her, her mouth twisted and shifting as if attempting to speak to her.

In this appearance, the face did not devolve like usual, but it hovered over her own and remained. Ashley felt the flesh of her arms rise with a shiver under the woman's unwavering eye contact. Her eyes were dark and deep and spilling over with disdain. Ashley opened her mouth and shook her head in an attempt to knock the face off of her and gasped when she saw that she still wore the woman's expression like a mask – her mouth frozen in a snarl. In a moment of panic, Ashley slapped herself and shut off the flashlight.

She sat in the dark of the attic for seconds that seemed to stretch on for years, while rolling waves of thunder continued to crash in the distance. She brought her hand to her mouth and felt the shape of her jaw and cheeks and lips, which all felt like her own. She wanted to leave the attic and return to her bedroom but could not find her way without the light. She picked the flashlight up from the ground but hesitated to turn it on in case she might reveal something that she did not want to see. She was alone when she entered the attic, but she had a distinct feeling that she was no longer by herself. No, there was something there with her – near her, hovering, breathing down her neck without breath.

She held the flashlight in her hands. *The light could reveal something bad*, she considered – *oh it will reveal something bad*. She hated the thought of what she might find in the light, still feeling that shadowed and haggard face hanging over her shoulder, whispering insanity into her ear.

Ashley moved her thumb to the switch and shut her eyes as she flicked it on. Slowly, she opened one eye after another only to realize that the flashlight no longer worked. No light shone. Instead, she sat in the darkness, barely able to make out the shadows around her until another flash of lightning lit the attic. In her reflection in the mirror, she saw the face of the woman behind her – the mask of a dark figure with a long and twisted mouth standing over her and rising. Ashley screamed under the roar of another wave of thunder as she scrambled on sheets of plywood, catching a spider web on her face.

She threw herself sideways – away from where the figure floated and away from the mirror. She felt a sharp pain bite at her leg and let out a yelp. *It was just a spider or a nail*, she reassured herself. She reached a hand out to feel her way towards the entrance of the attic – moving closer to the small square hole in the floor illuminated by the subtle glow of the hallway. "Please don't feel anything, please don't feel anything," she pleaded.

As she crept forward on her hands and knees, reaching her hand forward again and sifting through the air in front of her, a spider crawled across her fingers. She shook it with a sob escaping from her lips. Kneeling, she glanced over her shoulder at the mirror and was thankful that she couldn't see it in the dark. She continued shuffling her way forward until the ladder was in front of her.

She dangled her feet through the hole of the ceiling, terrified that someone – *something* – was in the hallway waiting for her. She couldn't shake the fact that, even without seeing anyone near her, she knew she was in company. It wasn't just the old woman; it was *all of them*. She was in a sea of swimming formless bodies, and she could feel them even if she could not see them.

Ashley shimmied down the ladder, sliding her hands down the sides and nearly losing her footing. Before her foot left the last peg, she was racing back to her bedroom, losing a slipper along the way. The hall never felt so long, seeming to stretch on and on as she dashed for her door and shut it behind her. The entrance to the attic was wide open, and the ladder was still set. Her parents would find it in the morning and ask questions, but there was no time to care about that. She needed to get out of there. She'll explain that she thought she heard a noise – a leak from the rain, maybe – and just wanted to check it out for herself. "Oh, it was nothing – but better safe than sorry," she'll tell them with a smile. But, for God's sake, was whatever happened in the attic confined to the attic? Would *they* follow her with the ladder down?

Ashley laid in her bed with her blankets pulled over her head. She was doing her best to feign that nothing was wrong and that she saw nothing in that mirror, but the experience was undeniable and she still felt *them – all of them*. Oh *they* did follow her – whoever or whatever *they* were – were with her. *They* were standing in her bedroom – poised at the foot of her bed and hovering over her as she lay with her head pressed into her pillow, hidden under her blanket. Yes, *they* were there with her, crowding her in her bed. She could feel them breathing on her – their warm and humid breath pressing on her skin.

2

Mondays are hard enough to muster through in their own right, but this particular Monday was all the more challenging while moving through a fog of her bereavement. Her parents did not afford her the opportunity to stay home from school for a mental health day; that was the sort of thing they couldn't relate to. If they were sad, they somehow fought it away to the point that Ashley couldn't detect it. It seemed they had a tendency to actively fake their okayness in all sorts of life situations, utilizing an arsenal of false smiles and distant hugs. Maybe it was from being on the receiving end of their performances that Ashley found her passion for drama and her skill for acting.

A mental health day might have been good for her, and she weighed the idea of feigning sickness. But after the weirdness of everything that happened the night before, she didn't really feel like being stuck at home either. Then again, what *actually* happened last night? She moved like a zombie through her morning routine, making an effort to avoid the mirror in her bathroom as she got ready for her day.

"It's not Mondays that suck," Val suggested. "It's your life."

Usually, Ashley would have a counter-quip or a counter-punch, but it just wasn't there. She would bring up something about a disappointing TV show or the fight she was having with her parents about the role she was going to audition for in the upcoming school play. Or, maybe she would make some snide comment about her disgust with Mr. Sanchez for flirting with Tracy – the head cheerleader who sits front and center in their Social

Studies class. Today, all Ashley could do was shift her gaze from the bus window towards Val and smirk. In fact, that whole fight she had with her mom over the weekend about which roles she was "allowed" to audition for seemed to fall from her awareness altogether.

"OK, you don't have to get dramatical about it," Val said. She could see Ashley's defeat and acknowledge it, and they rode the bus in a comfortable silence.

The whole way to school, Ashley couldn't focus on anything other than what happened last night. She played with the idea of telling Val about it, because she was having a hard time talking about anything else, but she was afraid Val would think she was having some kind of mental breakdown. Fortunately, the bus was running late to get to school, and there wasn't much downtime before the bell rang anyway.

Ashley made her way from her locker to Social Studies and took her assigned seat. After attendance, Mr. Sanchez allowed her to go to the nurse. She had a reputation for being a solid and reliable student, and Ashley was appreciative of the benefits that came with that reputation when she needed them – like being allowed to go to the nurse's office when you're not feeling well.

Instead of going straight there, she loitered in the hallway and pulled out her cell phone. She wanted to know if what she remembered happening the night before had actually happened, or if it was some weird lucid dreaming thing. According to a few different websites, it might've been something as harmless as a waking-dream, where even though you're awake, part of your brain is still dreaming, and you have trouble differentiating dream from reality. It would make sense; she was tired and it was the middle of the night when everything happened – when her brain was used to dreaming anyway. And, she was under a lot of stress, she reminded herself. She wrestled with those redeeming qualifiers and did her best to hang onto them in order to dismiss the whole thing. When she had first awoke, she had hoped she hadn't even been in the attic at all and that it was a dream altogether, but her father yelling about the ladder to the attic being down robbed her of that wish. Part of her was afraid she would be robbed of this wish too.

Indeed, she made her way from the hallway towards the nurses office and paused in front of the window of a dark classroom. It was a complete accident, and she didn't mean to look in the reflection of the window. But she saw it. The hovering face of the haggard woman was standing behind her. Ashley muffled a cry and ran instinctively to the nearest bathroom. As she made her way in, she turned her head from the mirrors and darted into the closest stall. She was alone there and she could cry, already beginning to sob before she gave herself permission.

In a moment of frustration, she took her cell phone out of her pocket and held it up in front of her to see herself. Her hands were shaking, and she had a hard time steadying it. She was too afraid to look at her image in the phone and decided that she would take a picture and look at that instead. With her head turned to the side and crying into the corner of her shoulder, she clicked away a series of selfies. When she finished, she bobbled her phone in her unsteady hands looking to find the pictures she took.

The first one entirely missed her and only showed the top of the stall behind her. In the next, she caught a piece of her right shoulder and a dark shadow hanging behind her. The third one though, that one was square on. The image caught her with her head turned to the side, crying into her arm. Looking directly at her was the haggard woman – dark hair disheveled and hanging all over Ashley. The woman's mouth was open, showing a long tongue reaching towards Ashley's forehead.

At the sight of the image, Ashley let out a horrific howling cry and began weeping. "Leave me the fuck alone!" she screamed. Her voice echoed off the walls of the bathroom and back at her.

Ashley buried her face into her open hands and continued to cry, feeling a blend of hopelessness and helplessness. It's not like she could tell the school nurse about her problem. She couldn't call the police about a malevolent spirit. Her friends would think she should be institutionalized. The only person who might have listened to her would have been her grandmother, and she was dead.

In a moment of clarity, Ashley brought her phone out again and went back to the website where she learned how to contact the spirits. She left a post about her situation and the haggard woman who was following her. She could only hope someone might know what to do about it.

By the time she finished posting on the site, she had calmed down enough to feel more like herself. The next step was to leave the bathroom without looking in the mirror. When she felt like enough time had gone by for her face to not appear puffy or her eyes like they had been crying, she opened the door to the stall with her chin down to her chest. She made a hard left for the bathroom door, as if the mirror were watching her, judging her – condemning her.

Upon leaving the bathroom, Ashley failed to find a reason to return to class. She stood in the hallway, far and away from any dark classroom windows, and considered ideas for where to go and what to do next. She had never ditched class or school before, but if she were ever going to, this would be the time – after attendance was taken and right before the bell for the next class. She made her way to the exit by the art hallway. The door didn't have an alarm, and there wouldn't be any staff watching the hall.

As she pushed the door open, she walked out into the parking lot with a quick glance over her shoulder. It was the first time that she *could* reasonably get into trouble for doing something wrong at school. There was the time she got a detention for carrying an open yogurt container out of the cafeteria, but she didn't think that counted. Even her parents laughed about that.

Once she made it to the parking lot, she started to pick up her pace. It was doubtful anyone was monitoring the lot, but for as long as the school could make an extra dollar ticketing students with expired parking passes, they absolutely would. And, should they find a runaway student, they would find a way to fine her too. *I would have made for a good delinquent student*, she thought.

After clearing the parking lot and school property, Ashley jogged across the street and started walking towards the town's library. It seemed as good of a place as any to find out what was following her and what might happen to her.

The street seemed infinitely longer having to walk it than it ever felt as a passenger in a car. By walking, she was seeing things that she never noticed from the car – the types of trees, the condition of the houses on the street, even some small shops that she never really knew existed before. It was like she acquired a pass to enter a secret world – the lives that exist outside of a high school in the early afternoon.

As she made her way down the street, she came across a white shack with a neon "Psychic" sign in the window. There were no cars in the small driveway for the place, which was likely an old house that someone turned over into their psychic headquarters. Normally, Ashley wouldn't waste her time or money on a psychic, but she was uncovering new worlds, new beliefs, and if anyone might understand what she was going through, it might be a psychic. Then again, the type of people who ticket students at school or buy new suits with the money from the collection plate at church (which was a well known transaction at her parents' church) might also be the kind of people who run a psychic shop.

Ashley made her way up the long tar driveway, noting how average the house appeared despite its rundown condition. *And what did you expect, fairies in the garden?*

As soon as she opened the door, she was taken aback by the smell of burning sage. What must have once been a foyer was now a small shop. A long glass counter stood before her. A cash register sat to the right, and to the left was a small old TV with crooked antennas playing some kind of black and white horror movie from the '50s. The glass case itself held various statues, crystals, stones, and herbal items – some labeled for strengthening communication with guiding angels, and others labeled to enhance one's libido. A threadbare tapestry hung from the wall behind the counter, its colors contrasting the worn blue carpeting. Ashley followed the foot trail to a room on the right. So far, no mirrors, and she was glad for that.

The next room over was illuminated by tacky green and purple lights lining the ceiling – the kind that go on sale around Halloween time. A woman sat in a large chair at a round table covered in a red cloth. She pulled her dark hair back and locked it behind her ear.

"Hello, child. Please, come in," the woman welcomed with a smile, motioning to the open seat. It was a peculiar greeting, Ashley thought, but it fit in line with what she expected. Whether the spectacle was real or show though, well, that was yet to be determined.

"Hi," Ashley returned timidly.

"Don't be afraid, darling. I don't bite," the woman said with a grin, revealing a handful of gold plated teeth. She had some kind of accent that Ashley couldn't place. A poor impression of something Romanian, perhaps.

"I've never really done this before," Ashley confessed. She stared at the gray streak in the lady's long and wavy black hair. She was having a difficult time deciding if the woman was in her late twenties or her early sixties – or anywhere in-between.

"That's OK, dear. Do you want tarot reading?" the woman asked.

"I don't know, I…" Ashley trailed off.

"You want palm reading?" the lady continued.

"No," Ashley started. "I think I have something bad following me."

"Something bad?" The lady raised her eyebrows with intrigue. "Tell me."

Ashley started from the beginning – not just the night in the attic, but the whole thing. She talked about how close she was with her grandmother – their inside jokes, their long talks over the phone, and the surprise of finding out that she passed away in her sleep. There was shock there, even though everyone saw it coming for months with her diminishing health – the way her hands shook harder and how her memory started to have more bad days than good ones, but that didn't make it any better. Ashley just needed to talk to her one last time – just one last time to tell her she loved her and one last time to tell her that she would miss her. The truth of it was, she couldn't remember how she hung up from her last phone call with her, and too many days went by between that phone call and the visit that came before it. The real truth of it was, she didn't show her grandmother how much she loved her in her last weeks – maybe even months; it was just too much.

"Your grandmother was special for you," the lady responded. The corners of her eyes shined back at Ashley. "Very special woman," she nodded.

"And, I got so desperate to talk to her again that I did something stupid," Ashley confessed. She went on about the night in the attic – the research that went into learning how to contact the dead, finding an item that belonged to the person (which, also happened to be a mirror – the second thing she needed), and waiting for a rainstorm so that the electrons in the air vibrated at a frequency conducive for making contact between parallel planes.

The psychic interrupted her with laughter. "You try too hard!" she exclaimed. "Your grandmother sees you, hears you," she paused, "just talk to her. She listens."

"But, how do I know?" Ashley asked. "How do I know

that she hears me?"

"You try too hard!" the lady exclaimed again with a warm smile. "She hears you. You can't hear her. Because you don't accept that she has moved on."

"But–" Ashley started.

"Listen," the lady instructed, "your grandmother moved on. No heaven, no hell. But she moved on. "

"Why isn't she in heaven?" Ashley asked.

"No heaven – just afterlife," she responded.

"What about hell?" Ashley asked.

"No hell," the lady replied. "All spirits go to the afterlife. Some spirits are lost and take longer to find it. But your grandmother is not lost."

"Then what is this thing following me? This old woman – you don't understand!" Ashley's lip started to quiver. She reached into her pocked to take out her cell phone. "Look, do you have a mirror? I'll show you."

"No mirror," the lady replied and put her hand over Ashley's hand with her phone. "No pictures," she continued. "Ignore it."

"Ignore it?" Ashley asked. "How can I…"

"Ignore it," the woman repeated. She leaned back with folded arms. "Ignore it, ignore it, ignore it!"

"Can she hurt me?" Ashley asked.

"Not yet," she paused, looking at her hands for her words. "Lost spirits are weak. They are around us all of the time, but they cannot hurt you if you ignore them."

Ashley started to smile for the first time in days, and she longed to go home and to go back to school tomorrow – ready to give up her burden of fear. She imagined that by the time she got home, her parents would still be at work. A note might be left on the kitchen table in her dad's handwriting, cautioning her that the storm had knocked out the power in the neighborhood, "So don't leave the fridge open for longer than necessary," it would say.

Instead of heading off to her bedroom to start her homework, she would sit in the kitchen for a while, noticing the sun going down earlier than it did the week or even days before. She would contemplate that summer had officially ended when school started, but that the way the leaves piled up at the window sill was the real marker for the end of summer. She would think about how she hadn't even noticed the trees changing color this year, and it was like one day she was swimming in Val's backyard and the next she was hanging her collection of hoodies in her closet to prepare for fall.

The rest of the late afternoon and early evening would be unremarkable. Her parents would come home, bringing a rotisserie chicken with them. After dinner, her father would reset all the clocks in the house with the power back on, and he'd set his turntable to play a series of '50s doo-wop hits that would go on into the night. Meanwhile, her mother would spend the night reading in the kitchen. And, as for herself, she would spend the night avoiding all of the mirrors in the house. "Just ignore it," she would repeat out loud.

Her bathroom was the one in the upstairs hallway, just across from her bedroom and approximately six walking-paced footsteps from the entrance to the attic (she measured it). She had been to a variety of bathrooms since the previous night, but she found she could avoid looking in the mirror by keeping her gaze fixed on things at the side of the room – a window, a towel rack, a tacky piece of bathroom art. And, she would do that tonight, too.

She imagined herself standing at the entrance of the bathroom and reaching her arm inside to turn on the lights. Even if she could *ignore it*, there was no way she would go into the bathroom if the lights were not working. She would find a way to go in a bottle if she had to, but no bathrooms without lights.

But, the lights would work! So, she would walk into the bathroom, her footsteps syncopated with the '50s bass lines playing downstairs, and her eyes fixed on the towel rack above the toilet. She would reach her hands into the sink with her head turned to the right, reassuring herself that if she were to turn towards the mirror, there would be nothing there but her own reflection. *Ignore it!* Keeping her head still, she would glance at the mirror out of the corner of her eyes and see the side of her face, and it would be *her face*. "All right, Ash, let's chill out," she would whisper to herself. She would turn her head to face the mirror and find herself greeted by her own reflection. She would let out a sigh of relief and a small chuckle, perfectly timed with someone's "whoah-oh-ohhh" from her father's stereo.

In this daydream, she would be reminded of her wash up routine as a little girl back when her grandmother would stay over at her parents' house for the holidays. Even then, her father's old music would maneuver its way upstairs and into the bathroom. She remembered the way she would glance at herself in the bathroom mirror, fiddling with her hair – red bows working overtime to hold two ponytails in place – while she bounced her knees and sang along to cheesy love songs.

She would remember the way she used to take a drop of soap between her palms and a splash of warm water from the running faucet and press her hands together before drawing them apart. She would remember the diamond between her thumbs and index fingers showing a rainbow of soap colors and how she would blow a kiss at the diamond as she brought her hands together – leaving a soap bubble of her kiss to fly through the air. She would remember how she used to hear her grandmother laugh from the doorway – that hearty and unrestrained contagious laugh. Ashley would chuckle just thinking about it, and she would bring her hands together the way she did as a little girl, making another soap diamond, and blow a kiss into it and send it into the air. It would fly from her hands and through the doorway to the hall – hovering in the air for just seconds before popping where it once landed on her grandmother's cheek.

"But," the psychic went on, "if you pay attention to them, they grow strong."

Ashley shook her head and knocked the daydream from her mind. "So how do I know how strong or weak she is? I've been paying a lot of attention to her!" Ashley exclaimed. "I want to stop her so that she can't come after me," Ashley said.

The psychic let out a sigh and leaned forward before continuing. "She will not go away. Death is around you. But you cannot fight it, or you give a microphone to a whisper." The woman waited for her words to register on Ashley's face. "You are sad? So OK, be sad," she shrugged. "You think about death too much. You are alive. Be alive until you no longer are."

Ashley looked at her, scanning the woman's face. There was a gentleness in her eyes. "You do believe me, don't you?" Ashley asked.

"I do. You contacted the dead – no doubt. But they feed on the energy you spend on them, so no more feeding – no more fighting."

Ashley looked down at her phone, she wanted to delete all the selfies she took at school, but she also didn't want to see the pictures anymore. She took her phone out and handed it to the psychic. "Here, I took some pictures of her, and I don't want to see them. Can you delete them for me? They're just the last three pictures I took."

The psychic took the phone from Ashley and opened up the camera. She moved matter-of-factly, swiping her fingers across the phone. First, she deleted one picture and then the next. But when she came to the third picture, she froze. She dropped the phone onto the table and pushed her chair back with her air stuck in her throat.

"What's wrong?!" Ashley asked.

The psychic shook her head slowly with her eyes wide open, gradually moving her head faster and faster. "No," she said.

"What is it!? What's wrong?!" Ashley asked again. She

reached across the table for the phone as the psychic continued to push her chair backwards into the corner of the room.

"You must go!" the psychic commanded.

"What is it?! What happened?!" Ashley grabbed the phone and saw the same horrid picture as before. She was pressed against the toilet, leaning away from the camera with her face hidden into her left arm. And, opposite her arm, the side of the haggard old woman's face – her hair tasseled and hanging in all directions over herself and Ashley, her long and burning tongue reaching out of her open mouth and chasing Ashley's forehead.

"I cannot help you. I am sorry. You must go," the psychic repeated. "Go!" she said again, louder.

"But what's wrong?! What do I do?" Ashley asked, pleading with the psychic, starting to cry again.

"There is nothing you can do. You should not have contacted the dead. She has found you, and you must go," the psychic repeated again.

"Who?! Who is she?!" Ashley asked, pleading again for an answer.

"She is moroaică – a hag!" the psychic shrieked.

"A hag?!" Ashley yelled in return.

"Yes, she is a very sad and angry spirit." The psychic let out a shriek before beginning to cry, "Oh, she is speaking to me."

"What does she want?!" Ashley asked between her own choked sobs.

"She is yelling at me! She is so angry, so hurt, so afraid!"

"Why me?! What did I do?" Ashley asked.

"She wants your life – your breath," the psychic replied. "She believes she can return to life through you."

"But why me?!" Ashley shrieked again.

"She found her way to this world through you. She heeded your call."

3

Ashley ran out of the psychic's house screaming, and she continued to scream at the top of her lungs as she ran home. Her feet tripped over themselves as she sprinted.

Passing the reflections of windows in houses and storefronts, she saw the hag not behind her or near her, but in the reflections themselves. In one window, she was a face hiding in shadows, her hair flailing around her in the wind. In another window, she was an arm reaching through the reflection, grasping for Ashley. In other reflections, she watched Ashley – opening and closing her mouth after her, as if she might somehow bite her through a window.

Ashley continued to make her way home, hoping to arrive before her parents. She ran through backyards and dodged cars that drove past her – not for the danger of them striking her, but for the haggard woman who sat within every window of every passing vehicle.

Once she made it home, she had a plan. It was a wild one and perhaps her only chance for survival. But, no matter what, she would not *ignore it*; there was no way she was living with this thing following her forever. If this hag wanted her life, she would have to take it. It all started with her grandmother's mirror, and perhaps it could end there too.

Ashley threw open the front door of her house and launched her book bag to the couch and made her way into the garage. She glanced at the reflection in the family room TV as she made her way, noticing the woman's steady gaze. A shiver ran down Ashley's spine.

In the garage, she took her father's hammer from his toolbox and marched upstairs to the attic. There was no hesitation in her step, and her plan might only work if she never stopped to consider its recklessness.

Upon reaching the attic, she pulled the ladder down, ignoring its groan and protest. She made her way through the ceiling and crouched on a plywood board. The light from outside was dim, but it was enough to find the pristine, cloth-covered mountain she was looking for. She presumed she was safe, so long as it was covered. She would have to thank her dad for doing that.

She crawled across cracked plywood boards, swiping at nails and knocking them from her path. A series of low whispers called to her from behind the cloth. If what the psychic had explained to her was true, the hag was harmless when she first met her because she wasn't strong enough to do anything other than get close to her. But by now, she might be an actual force to be reckoned with.

Ashley approached the mirror with her hammer in hand. She reached up and brought it down over the cloth covered surface, striking it again and again and again – each swing producing a muffled sound of cracking and shattering glass. And just like that, it was done. Ashley reached for the cloth and tore it from the mirror ready to strike once more. Alas, the mirror was empty except for several shards of cracked glass hanging in place. There was no woman – no reflection except for one of herself kneeling on the attic floor, the hammer pulsing in her hand.

Ashley took a deep breath and let it out with a sigh of relief. With the hammer still in hand, she reached forward and knocked the last remaining shards of glass to the attic floor. She would have to explain the destruction to her parents as an accident, but the idea of being grounded for such a thing even seemed funny to her – like yogurt in the hallway. She would take the punishment in stride.

She turned around to crawl towards the ladder when she was stopped dead in her tracks. The old and haggard woman was full bodied in a black dress that started and ended in shadows. Her long and twisted hair raised from her head and danced in the air like smoke. Ashley screamed with the remaining scratched voice she had left and fell backwards into the mirror.

The old haggard woman crept steadily towards her, moving and creaking the floorboards as she hobbled on thin bony legs from beneath her dress. Her arms protruded from her center, her long and misshapen fingers reaching for Ashley. They made their way to Ashley's neck, holding her in place. Ashley shook her head from side to side, crying to herself in silence.

She laid on the ground, choking, as the hag brought her face to Ashley's ear, whispering her insanity at her. There were no coherent words, just a sensation of numbing, as if her brain were catching some kind of frostbite.

The hag slithered her tongue at Ashley, inserting it into her mouth and down her throat. Ashley gagged and choked as it made its way down into her. Her arms and legs wriggled and writhed, but nothing she did could stop the hag from taking her life. She believed this was death, and she wrestled her way through the timeless blackness. But, eventually, the fight left her, and she lay still with the hag's frostbite gnawing at her brain.

4

This is death, Ashley thought. That is, until she opened her eyes and found that she was not dead at all. Rather, she was gazing out into the attic from behind a cracked and clouded glass veil. Everything before her was backwards from the way she remembered it. Ashley saw the hag seated in front of her. But she looked different now – changed in someway. She was devolving, growing youthful – her face's contours shifting over themselves the way they did when Ashley stared into the mirror to contact the dead.

The hag maintained her unwavering eye contact with Ashley as she grew younger, her skin becoming taut, soft, and smooth, until, finally, Ashley saw a mirror image of herself.

Ashley watched as she saw the hag – this other self –

raise her hands to her face, feeling her cheeks and mouth and neck. Ashley's own arms mimicked the movements, as if compelled by an imaginary puppeteer to do exactly as the hag did. Her mirrored image twirled in a circle and so did she.

Ashley's father called to her (to them) from downstairs, "Ash, honey, dinner time! Come to the kitchen like a good girl!" The bass line of a doo-wop song followed in the wake of his voice.

She wished to call back, to scream to him for help. But, instead, her mouth followed the movements of this other version of herself, "Be right down in a second, dad!" she heard herself yell.

"That's my girl!" he returned.

Compelled in her movements, Ashley found herself dancing to her father's music, bobbing her shoulders and swaying, like a body possessed. In coordination with her other self on the other side of the glass veil, she picked up what appeared to be a small shard of reflective glass, which was then gently placed in the center of her grandmother's cheval mirror, cracked and pieced back together like a puzzle.

"Just like new," the hag said, and leaned forward to kiss Ashley's lips on the other side of the fractured mirror. Ashley was made to smile in return.

"Love you, dad!" she heard herself call downstairs, her lips tracing the hag's words.

The hag reached down – and Ashley followed – to pick up the white cloth on the ground. Ashley watched on and helplessly placed the cloth on her side of the mirror, matching the perverted copy of herself.

The white cloth fell over the mirror, and Ashley's sight was covered in darkness.

MARVIN'S TAVERN

Marvin's Tavern stands somewhat crooked and has for about as long as anyone can remember. The plaque hanging near the front door says it was built sometime in the late 1800's, and once you're inside, it sounds every bit its age with all of its creaks and groans. It's old, scenic maybe – with a long lake at its back – but it's not remarkable. If you didn't know to look for it, you might not even find it. It's kind of like a man pointed to a hill on a whim one day and thought to clear a space between the trees and to build a bar there. I suppose that is what happened, and that man's name was Marvin.

Marvin was something of a local legend – fame or infamy, maybe a little bit of both. In its prime, Marvin's Tavern was an evening fixture – a place to stop for a drink or to end your night. Marvin would serve as bartender while catching up with the local folk about the latest happenings. They hung a photograph of him in the bar from his younger days, where he's wiping down some glasses, his serious expression hidden behind a formidable mustache.

He only had one child, a son named Maurice. From what I understand, Marvin's wife, Beth, was killed in a horse and buggy accident some years into Maurice's childhood. Some say it was a highway robbery, and that she was targeted as Marvin's wealthy wife. Others say that *she* was actually the one doing the robbing. Verdict was never really reached on that one. Either way, Marvin wouldn't remarry or seek out other female company, claiming that she was his one and only true love. He brought up her smile any opportunity he could and even commissioned an artist to paint a picture of her in mid-laugh – uncommon for the time. He hung the picture behind the bar where I imagine it still sits today – a bit dusty and a bit worn, maybe.

Maurice didn't have the charm that his father had. He was born deaf, which made it hard for him to make friends. He could lip read and understand others well-enough, but he had a real bad speech impediment. The town folk would talk about him behind his back and make their jokes, but no matter their gossip, he had a way with tools and carpentry that silenced even the cruelest of town critics.

Thing about Maurice was, being deaf and all, Marvin learned to became real protective of him, making sure that no boy of his would be seen as a town fool. He would harass the boys and girls that came near the tavern, just assuming they were there to mock Maurice. So, eventually, some of the local boys thought to get a little payback at Marvin's expense. They came into the bar one afternoon when Maurice was by himself, and a few jokes turned into an all out fight. From what legend says, the boys were making fun – earning their trouble that Marvin was giving them anyway – when Maurice tried to defend himself. He might've gotten a few good swings in, but he was outnumbered, and they managed to get his arms behind his back, and they pinned him to the ground. A real sick bunch these kids were. While he was held down, the leader of the group took a knife from the bar and cut Maurice's ears off. "You don't use 'em anyway!" he cackled.

Well, when Marvin returned to the bar, the boys were

standing over Maurice, laughing and holding his ears up to his head and taking them on and off again. Grasping the scene, Marvin took the claw side of a hammer and caught the leader in the back with it. While the rest of them were scuffling out of there, he also caught one of the slower ones by the hair. They say the boys' faces were unrecognizable when they were found. Neither of them survived, and that changed public opinion of Marvin – not that it was too high to begin with.

The dead boys' fathers came back to the bar that night with a few other men and intended to kill Marvin, eye for an eye kind of stuff. Something snapped in him and, according to the survivors from that night, Marvin wrestled two of them to the ground and strangled them to death one-handed each. He fought off another one of the men, shattering his face in different places. That man died from his injuries some days later.

The boys may have started the fight, but Marvin sure finished it. Some suspected the police would arrest Marvin, but for one reason or another, they hardly investigated the murders. Some said that Marvin had them all in his pocket, and others said that what Marvin did was just – simple as that. Either way, it wasn't good for business, and the toll it took on Marvin seemed to accelerate his aging.

In his last years, Marvin's black mustache had turned white along with his wild eyebrows. He would hobble around hunched over, muttering about his body falling apart. Something in the bar would need repair, and despite his best efforts to attend to the issue, he would be asked to step aside while Maurice did the fixing. He spent his final years trading glances between his painting of his laughing Beth and his own wrinkled and shaking hands.

After the controversy, there were no more customers for the bar, but it couldn't have happened at a better time, as prohibition was just getting started. Some thought that would be the end of Marvin's Tavern, but apparently the two men managed to find a new line of revenue to keep the place afloat. No one could quite figure out what it was – weekends, weeknights, out of town characters would show up dressed to the nines to close the place out. Everyone just assumed they were liquoring up the cops or paying forward political favors.

At the same time, they say Marvin passed away in a falling accident in the bar's cellar, and Maurice had something like a mental breakdown and became a recluse thereafter – seen less and less often outside the bar until he seemed to disappear altogether.

Towards the end of those years, just about everyone in town had forgiven Marvin's nefarious history and connection to the place, well, except for the last of those boys' fathers. Just as business started rolling again, he threw a bottle bomb through a window and set the place on fire. He admitted his guilt and didn't fight the charges, though he wouldn't discuss what compelled him to do it. Some considerable damage was done, including handfuls of deaths, but nothing to wipe the place away completely.

Marvin's Tavern really is the best kept secret in town, and its complicated past splits public opinion on it – either the town folk frequent it, or they change the conversation when you talk about it.

The first time I saw the place, my girlfriend and I had spent the night out drinking at the lake under the hill – just blowing off steam on spring break. We had this little wooden raft that we'd throw out into the water and drift around on until we returned to shore. It was the kind of thing we'd done a hundred times before, but that night we ended up in a spat. She told me that she got accepted into a program for teaching abroad, and she was talking about how she was going to live her dream of teaching English to kids from other countries and whatnot. And, I don't know, something about the idea of her going off to another country while I waited for her to come home – failing out of my gen ed classes in the meantime – I guess I snapped.

We were screaming at each other, and I was yelling that I wouldn't let her leave me. One thing led to another, and before I knew it, I had my hands on her. I was squeezing her neck and watching her change colors — starting to wonder if her head might pop off — when her knee came up and struck me in the groin. I rolled off of her so fast that I accidently tipped the raft and knocked us into the water. While I was trying to right the thing, she swam her ass to shore — probably for the best. I could hardly stay afloat, so I gave up and headed to shore too. But, I was all turned around, and I came out right at the base of the hill. Anyway, after I made it out of the water, I thought to go up and over the hill to the main road rather than taking the long trek back around the lake. Sure enough, as I crept over the top of the hill, there was Marvin's Tavern in all of her glory. And, God, did I need a drink.

That night and for the rest of my spring break, I drank and made a nook for myself amongst the locals, learning the sordid history of the place. But that bar, she's a deceptive one; having a drink there was like having a drink in your own grandmother's living room, if only your grandmother's house were built over Satan's den.

2

The funny thing about having a drinking problem is that the details — those little facts, the pieces of truth on wheels — seem to always be rolling away when you reach for them. When I look at the few details I managed to hang onto from my last night at Marvin's, the picture they paint is a bleak one.

I was thinking about calling Nicki — you know, trying to find a way to make things right — and I wanted to be sure I was in the right headspace for that kind of a conversation. I was parked at the wobbliest stool just a little bit right of center at the bar with my favorite bartender, Ellie. One lesson my foster dad taught me early on was that when you're going for something, "Go all in and go in good company." Ellie was about as good of company as you could find.

She looked like she was in her late twenties, but she would tell you stories about what her twenties were like when she lived them more than twenty years ago. Some people hire a shrink to talk to. Me? I had Ellie. Like her drinks, her words of wisdom packed a punch, and, let me tell you, you don't learn to swing like that until you've been around the block a bit.

Next to Ellie was my favorite new drinking buddy, Hank. Under that gruff beard of his was always a frown, but I swear he meant it like a smile. He was the sort of guy you'd fear breaking into your house in the middle of the night with a shotgun or something. I liked to remind him that that was why he would probably die alone; his goddamned beard scared away the women. He'd thank me for the advice, calling me a "motherless son of a bitch" in return – but always with a pat on the back.

So, there we were finishing our first round of drinks when Hank thought to ask Ellie for something special. After some consideration, Ellie poured him something she called, "Death in the Afternoon."

"Listen, absinthe gets a bad rap, but it makes for a nice night. You just enjoy the drink and don't tell anyone who poured it," Ellie explained. "Capisce?"

"Capisce," Hank said with a wink.

"Hey Ellie, what if I wanted to try something a little less *safe*?" I asked.

"I think a little 'Death in the Afternoon' would do you just fine, too," she replied.

"No, I mean, that's good and all," I began, "but you've made me that before. What would you be pouring for you, if you were me?"

"You really want to know what I would make for me?"

"Yeah, what would that be?" I asked.

"You really want to go for it, huh?" Ellie asked. She

paused, tilted her head, and let out a deep sigh.

"Absolutely. Give me something ominous," I said.

"Listen, if you think you're ready for it, I've got something for you. But I'm only making you one, and if you tell anyone about it, I'll deny it."

"Shit, Ellie, what's in it?" I asked.

Without answering, Ellie grabbed a glass from the counter and took it behind a closed door in the back. I turned to Hank, "Is she serious?" I asked.

"I've learned to not mess with her," Hank chuckled.

Ellie returned from the room with a miniscule amount of some kind of foaming liquid in the bottom of a glass. She proceeded to mix a few other bottles into it and then slid it across the counter to me.

"Listen, Ryan, you drink this slow, and just enjoy the ride," she cautioned.

"What is it?" I asked.

"It's a family secret," she winked. "I only give it to my favorites, and it comes with a coffee at the end of the night so you can tell me all about it."

I held the glass in my hand and swirled the drink a couple of times, imagining that I knew what to do to appreciate it. It had a pungent odor to it; something was hiding under the smell of the other liquors – tequila and whiskey, I think they were. I put it to my lips and noticed nothing unusual except for the taste. If drinking scotch had hints of smoke flavoring, then this was like drinking dirty rainwater out of a fire pit.

"Wow, Ellie, this is awful! This is what you make for your favorites? I want my money back," I joked.

"Just take it slow, young blood," she smiled.

"Want a sip?" I asked Hank.

He waved my offer off with his hand. "Ellie's already made me one of those. One was enough," he chuckled.

Hank must've had five or six drinks before I finished my first. We played a game of chicken to see who'd be the first to have to get up to hit the John. I don't remember the score that night, but Hank was the first to break the seal. By the time I had to go, I was a bit off balance to say the least.

I hobbled my way to the bathroom, bracing myself against the wall on my way there, careful to not tear down any of the fraying wallpaper. Once I got to the door, I kind of fell inside. Now, I went in there to take a leak, but I couldn't find the urinals – like they were all taken off the wall or something and replaced with stalls. I don't like to make a habit of sitting in public restrooms, but settling for a stall didn't seem like such a bad idea in my condition. It was only then, when I was already sitting down, that I realized I was in the women's restroom. That was all right though, it would make for a funny story to remember the night by – something to add to a future catalogue of "Remember that time when…." But, that was the last part of the night that resembled any kind of normalcy.

I was considering leaving the stall to head to the men's room when the bathroom door swung open. A woman walked in wearing a bright green dress that clung to the best curves on her body, and she carried a small bag with her. I peaked out from the crack between the stall and the door to see her remove some kind of black band and feather from her head. I didn't mean to be watching her, but I couldn't leave the stall either; the last thing I wanted was for someone to call the cops about a pervert hanging out in the women's bathroom. I tucked my legs onto the toilet and sat as quietly as I could while waiting for her to leave.

But, instead of leaving, two more women came in after her – each one just as stunning as the first, and each with her own cloth bag. The second woman wore a red dress with tassels and had multiple layers of white pearls hanging from her neck. The third woman wore a black dress – the shortest one – that seemed to have gold chains dangling from it. My first impression was that these women must have been celebrities or movie stars, but what would they be doing at Marvin's Tavern?

The three women watched themselves in the mirror while removing their ornate pieces of jewelry and headbands, placing them with care into the small bags that they had brought with them. They didn't speak or even acknowledge one another as they continued to remove pieces of their outfits. I thought to say something to allow myself to leave – something to clarify that I accidently slipped into their bathroom.

The woman in green reached to the bottom of her dress and pulled it up over her head, exposing her bare body with exception to her underwear and bra. I wish I could say I had the decency to look away, but I did not. Aside from admiring her form, I was taken aback by the design of her undergarments. Believe me, I had seen enough women in different styles of underwear before to know that what she was wearing was strange; she was like a vintage model. The woman in red removed her dress next, revealing something like a tight nightgown. The woman in black, too, wore some kind of slip beneath her dress. Each of them removed those layers as well and placed them in their bags.

The three women stood momentarily naked and beautiful in front of the bathroom mirror in silence – neither acknowledging or speaking to one another. Next, the one that had been wearing a green dress, brought her hand to her face and looked to be digging her nails into her skin under her jaw. I put my hand over my mouth to keep from gasping as I saw little trails of blood drip down her arms. I wanted to burst from the stall to stop her from hurting herself, but the other two women started doing the same thing. They each pulled the skin back from under their jaws and unraveled the flesh from their faces. They were muscle-tissued and red. Systematically, as if going through routine, each of them continued to skin their bodies with their nails. Each made her way down her neck and shoulders and arms and torsos and legs, leaving a puddle of blood at their feet.

The room began to spin, and I thought I was going to pass out or vomit – maybe both. As much as I wished to look away, I was captivated by their grotesque bodies. After skinning themselves, the women reached into their bags for long black gowns and placed them over their bloodied masses, losing their form and figures under thick layers of robed cloth.

Last, each woman brought out a headpiece from their bag. They appeared to be long, black, tanned and leathered beaks – the kind of thing doctors wore during the black plague of the middle ages. The women placed the masks over their own faces, obscuring their mouths and expressions. Then they turned to one another and took turns securing them with laces and belt hooks. Each woman lifted her own hood from her robe, covering any remaining part of her face. Without words, they stood silently in front of the mirror and walked single file from the restroom.

Once they left, I stumbled my way out of the stall and crashed into the bathroom sink, having slipped on the trails of blood that coagulated into one pool of crimson. I thought to look through the women's bags but began to gag from their iron-laden smell. Dizzied, I pushed the bathroom door open and became lost in the hall. The entire bar had gone silent – no music, no chatter, no nothing.

I leaned on the wall for support and began to make my way in the dim hallway towards the bar. As I went, my hands traced the contours of the wall until the wall itself gave way with the weight of my body. Something like a secret door flew open from the wall, revealing a long set of wooden stairs, which I proceeded to tumble down head over heels.

I awoke at the bottom of the stairs with aches and pains shooting up my legs. It was dark, but I could make out a series of glowing candles flickering in a large circle. As my eyes adjusted, I could see a group of individuals in leathered beaks surrounding the configuration of candles. There appeared to be no edges between their robes and the darkness.

In the middle of the circle was the bent body of a man laying next to a skeleton. They rested on an etching that was carved into the ground. I thought to call for help, but could not find my words. By the time I could process what I was seeing, I realized I was shrieking and already scrambling to find my way up the stairs. In my raucous fumbling, one figure broke from the formation and removed the beak and hood from his head. The last image I have of the night was a skinless man without ears.

I told you, my memory of that night was bleak.

3

There are hangovers and there are hanged-overs. I woke up the next afternoon to a blistering fever, having somehow been passed out and up all night at the same time. The worst thing about a fever is that it makes your bones ache, your blood boils, and everything is sensitive to touch – like you have no skin.

I never did get that coffee from Ellie at the end of the night, or maybe I did and I didn't remember. I spent the next week or two as a zombie, just puking my brains out; I remember that. Classes and finals were missed, and before I knew it, I was a community college dropout with nothing to say to anybody – not hard to do when you grow up a foster kid, always a "son" with an unspoken asterisk.

In the days and weeks that followed, there had been thin stretches of sobriety, but there had also been profound stretches of walking the highway and kicking stones in a drunken stupor, like some kind of demented animal on the prowl. As weeks bled into months and years, I lost my home, my friends, and my so-called family. I never worked up the courage to talk to Nicki again either.

In those days well-before cell phones, it was easier to just disappear, and I made a habit of it. I did well to stay away from Marvin's though; the idea of going back was about as good of an idea as sending a werewolf to live on the moon.

But, eventually, I saw the thing I always hoped for and dreaded at the same time: a Property for Sale sign. Apparently Marvin's Tavern was going to disappear. I guess I decided that if there were ever a reason to go back, it was to say goodbye.

4

I took the long walk to Marvin's, trekking up the backside of the hill and taking my time to remember what it was like when I first found the place – my clothes soaked, my body exhausted, and totally out of breath. I couldn't decide if I hoped to find Ellie still working there. If she did still work there, would she even remember me, one of her *favorites*?

I made my way around to the front, admiring the construction that two hands had built, and two more hands maintained for so many years – at least in the places where you could see the original work. A cold sweat had started to break out on the back of my knees; I wasn't sure of what I was hoping to find or do when I opened the door. No, I knew the answer to that: have a drink.

Touching the doorknob, I remembered the image of Maurice – the bloodied man without ears from the cellar. He had taken up residence in the back parts of my mind over the years, a reminder that I might just be clinically insane. God knows what happened down there that night or what was in my drink. I turned the knob and had to kick it in a bit – stubborn as ever – making for more of an entrance than I intended. I closed the door behind me and was greeted with a round of applause from a variety of patrons – young and old – smiling and clapping.

"Hey, there he is, the guest of the hour!" one of them yelled. Similarly, men and woman across the bar gradually rose to their feet, continuing to clap for me.

I was dumbfounded by the reception I was receiving – half unsure if I was standing near someone else who recently arrived and deserved the celebration, and half wondering if I was hallucinating. I was most struck by the sameness of the place, as if I had walked into some kind of living, breathing, time capsule. The whole thing was like walking into a dream. I've been called delusional before, but I swear they were waiting for me.

Cheers continued to follow and deflate as I smirked and nodded, doing my best to hold back the sense of panic building in my chest. Something was wrong. Something was oh-so-very wrong.

"For you, Ryan!" a guy named Ed called out from the entrance of the bar. He lifted his drink and took s swig. I remembered him; he was the local dancing drunk.

"Oh, c'mon. What is this shit?" I muttered under my breath. I was ready for the Marvin's Tavern experiment to end immediately. I hustled to turn back to the door but was blocked by a couple wearing what looked like party clothes from the 1920's.

"It's for you, Ryan!" they answered with obscene smiles.

"How do you know my name?" I asked in a whisper. I shrank back, instinctively trying to distance myself from the attention. A pit of nausea rolled in my stomach, and I tried to make my way again for the door. But, no matter how I turned, the whole tavern seemed to bend and turn with me. The bar was the only way forward, giving me the feeling I had been drugged and dizzied.

A man seated at a booth tipped his hat to me. "Up there, Ryan," he said. He pointed to the stool a little right of center from the bar and nodded.

"Don't let them bother you. We're just happy to see you is all," another voice called out.

It was like someone stuck me on pause while everyone else around me was allowed to keep moving – drinking, cheering, celebrating. A woman in a navy blue dress approached me and gave me a kiss on the cheek. "Drink with us, Ryan," she said.

"Ye-yeah," I stuttered out, finding my voice. I scanned the room in detail, taking in the old worn wooden flooring and the pinstripe wallpaper still splitting at the edges. The odd assortment of customers in the bar looked to be attending something like a decade party with everyone in costumes from the 1920's and on. Regardless of their outfits, all eyes were on me, encouraging me to make my way towards the stool that seemed to be waiting for me. I walked to it with hesitation, skimming my hand against creaky old wooden tabletops along the way.

As I approached the bar and my old wobbly stool, I saw Ellie posted behind the counter – looking as young and spry and joyful as ever. We made eye contact and she patted the place at the bar in front of her. Something about her calmed the waves in my stomach.

"What'll it be tonight, young blood?" she asked with a smile.

"Whoa, hold on," I exclaimed with pause. "What in the hell is going on here?"

She laughed. "It's good to see you again, Ryan," she said.

"I mean it. What the hell is going on?" I stammered, looking at the countertop and back to Ellie. "And look at you, what is your secret?" I asked, dragging out the words.

"Just breathe, Rye Guy. Here's a gin and tonic. Let's ride that train for a while," she said.

I nodded, forcing a false sense of ease.

Ellie poured my drink, slid it to me and then took a swig off the bottle. "Don't tell," she said and winked.

"Yeah," I replied, still holding onto my grimace. How was it possible that this place, that these people could look so much the way I left them a decade or so ago? The question had me scrambling to make sense of my sanity.

"Nothing they can do to you now," the man to my left

said. It was Hank. I was so distracted by seeing Ellie, I didn't even realize he was sitting right there with me, looking not aged by a day since our last night together.

"Goddamn, Hank!" I reached over and shook his hand, surprising myself with my own enthusiasm.

"Goddamn yourself," he chuckled, still grasping my hand. "It's been too goddamned long." He gave my arm another shake.

I surveyed the place from over Hank's shoulder, focusing on a cluster of crooked pictures adorning the wall. Out of the corner of my eye, I caught a glimpse of Ellie watching me with a look of warmth and concern. A part of me wished to let my guard down, to admit that – despite my questions – it just felt good to be back.

"All right, let's have a round for Ryan here, a drink in his honor!" a man called from a table in the back.

"Cheers to that," a woman next to Hank said and took a sip of her beer. She was wearing a green dress that left me feeling unsettled – a reminder of the woman in the green dress from the night when everything unraveled. The resemblance was unsettling.

"Cheers!" Ellie returned.

I sat back firmly on my stool and took a sip from my drink. "I just don't understand any of this," I started. "How did you any of you know I'd be here? How do you all look the same?"

"We're just so happy you're finally here with us," Ellie smiled.

Hank nodded after taking a sip from his drink.

"Why is everyone saying that?" I asked with rising tension in my voice.

"C'mon Rye Guy. Don't be like that. This is your night," the woman in green encouraged.

"My night? I don't have a night." My frustration was building again with every statement that avoided my questions. Nothing made sense – the round of applause, everyone knowing that I'd be here. "How do you know my name?" I asked her. "How does everyone know my name?"

"Poor bloke's confused. Still doesn't know, does he?" a man replied from behind Ellie. He was reaching for a bottle on the top shelf behind the bar, presenting his back to me. "If he doesn't know, he can't see the world as it is," he continued, reviewing the handwritten label on the bottle in his hand.

"What are you talking about?" I asked.

He turned around and placed the bottle on the counter. Pound for pound and mustache for mustache, it was the man from the picture wiping down the glass; it was Marvin. "Should someone tell this poor bloke what happened?" he asked.

"This is impossible!" I yelled. "Y-you're impossible," I stuttered in disbelief. The pit of nausea in my stomach rose with immediacy. Something was brewing in my gut, and it was just moments away from pouring out of me.

Marvin placed two glasses beside the bottle. "Welcome to my tavern," he said with arms raised, presenting the bar to me.

"Maybe you should tell him," Hank suggested to Ellie.

"You can't be here," I muttered to Marvin, to Ellie – to all of them. The sensation in my stomach continued to churn.

Ellie let out a sigh. "Ryan, Ryan, Ryan," she said and sighed again.

I stared at her blankly, wondering if I would make it to the bathroom in time to throw up if I had to. Even if I could make it, I decided I'd rather puke all over the countertop than to see a bathroom in Marvin's Tavern ever again. "You can't be here," I repeated.

Marvin poured two drinks from his mystery bottle and pushed one towards me, taking a sip from the one he poured for himself.

"Is the bar closing?" I managed to ask, pushing the drink away. I don't know where that question came from, but it felt important to ask – otherwise, it was like I had fallen into a spider web.

"We *are* at the end of our lease, I guess you could say," Marvin returned with a laugh. He glanced to Ellie and waited for her to fill in the blanks.

Ellie caught Marvin's gaze and turned back to me. "We hoped the sign might get you to come back," she said. Ellie took a deep breath before continuing. "Do you really want to understand?" she asked.

I nodded. Every part of my body was crawling with dread. This was definitely an oh-so-very-bad idea to come back here. I had officially shipped a werewolf to the moon.

"The last night you were here, you asked me for a special drink. Do you remember that?" she asked.

I nodded.

Marvin pointed to the drink he poured me.

"So, I gave it to you," she explained, "but, the drink I made you was a concoction of sorts – something that allows the user to see through time and space. I was trying to break the news to you, hon, because I didn't think you knew."

I couldn't find my words. "Knew w-what?" I choked out.

"Well, that you're dead, hon," she continued.

I gasped for air and could find none. A rush of nausea in my stomach took over, pumping waves of vomit out of my mouth. But, it wasn't thick or heavy or acidic, it just looked like water.

Marvin grabbed my glass away with haste. "This," he said, "would've helped with that." An air of disappointment stood out in his voice.

"I'm sorry, Ryan," offered the woman in the green dress.

"But, but–" I stammered between bouts of heaving, looking to Hank.

"Yeah, Ryan. When you were out on the lake," Hank started, "I think you drowned." He put his hand on my shoulder and nodded quietly.

A trail of water drooled from the corner of my mouth.

"My tavern is for the dead. You can't find it unless you've already passed on," Marvin explained. His words pulled the wind from my lungs. The lights above bar wavered and burst with a blast of electricity, forcing me to shield my eyes from the raining broken glass. I turned back to Marvin; his neck looked like it had bent and broken sideways. He watched me from an impossible angle and smiled. "It burned down after the bottle bomb in the '20s," he continued. His voice was strained and pressured, attempting to speak at his contorted angle.

I turned my gaze to look back at Ellie. Her smile and warm cheeks were replaced by divots in her skin and gaping holes of missing flesh. I gasped and fell off of my barstool. As I hit the ground, the entire tavern devolved again. It was charred and black, and it smelled of death. Water again welled up into my throat and mouth.

"Old places like this, the Muslin curtains over the windows, they burn quick and easy," Marvin continued. "No fire escapes, no emergency lighting, just a bunch of burning people trying to pull open a jammed front door with bodies blocking the way." He struggled to make his voice heard through his crooked neck.

The top of the bar cracked and fell to the ground with a thud, sending smoke and ash into the air. I scrambled backwards on the floor and pushed away from them. Ellie was riddled with bullet holes and missing pieces of her body.

I crawled backwards, bumping into a man at a table. He was looking down at me with a grotesque smile, his teeth pressing through bubbling and decayed skin that hung melted over his mouth. "Here, let me give you a hand," he laughed. He extended his hand down to me, and it was nothing but burnt bone and tendons. His clothes had welded to his body, making it impossible to identify charred cloth from skin.

"But the people downstairs!" I managed to say. Water ran from my mouth with every word, choking my breath. "They were real!"

"No honey, not anymore. Not when you were seeing them," Ellie answered. "Places like this, they gather memories of the things that happened and they like to dwell on them from time to time. I was trying to show you the coven meetings that took place in the cellar during the prohibition years. I wanted to help you make sense of things – of me and my family." Blood sprayed from her mouth with her every word.

"Your family?" I asked through a series of muffled attempts. Water pooled in my mouth and nose.

Marvin put his arm around Ellie's vibrant corpse. "This is my Beth," he explained.

"Ellie is short for Elizabeth, Rye Guy," she replied. "And the memory of this place that I was showing you was *that night*. I wanted you to see. I wanted you to know!"

I looked back to Hank on his barstool. His beard was scorched, and his skin hung from his body like loose sheets drying in the wind. "It's true," he said. His eyes looked as if they had boiled in his skull and dripped down his cheeks.

"What night?!" I wanted to scream but couldn't get enough air into my lungs. I scooted myself back into another table and knocked a pile of bones to the floor. Footsteps approached from behind; it was the skinless man without ears from the basement. The muscles in his face pulled back a semblance of a smile.

"You met our boy, Maurie," Ellie went on. "During those prohibition years, after Marvin died, Maurie wanted so badly to have his family back, that he found a way to do it! Every night, he hosted coven meetings in the cellar. He gave of his flesh to resurrect his flesh – just like the others taught him to do, you understand?"

Maurice reached his red and fleshy hand down to me to pull me to my feet, but the strength had left my body and I fell back to the floor in my puddle of watery vomit.

"And he kept at it until we could return to him," Ellie went on. "But, by then," she chuckled, "there wasn't much of him left."

"W-what night?" I stammered again.

"The night Maurice finally succeeded!" Ellie answered. "The night we were *reborn*." A ball of maggots fell forth from one of the holes in her neck. I wanted to shriek but gagged instead.

"Oh, you'll get used to the pain of it," Marvin said in his cracked voice.

"Good to have you with us, Ryan," a voice called out from the front of the bar. It was Ed, smashed against the front door where he had been hoisting his beer bottle only moments ago. Burnt bodies littered the ground around him and on top of him.

"We didn't mean for you to find out like this," the woman in the green dress said. She stood and approached from behind Maurice. The skin was missing from her entire body. "I'm sorry, Rye," she offered.

I crawled to my feet and attempted to worm my way across the ash-laden ground towards the door. With every effort, the door seemed to stretch further away.

"How do you know my name?!" I choked through mouthfuls of water. "Why me?!"

The skinned lady continued towards me, wincing as her vulnerable flesh made contact with ash floating through the air. Maurice joined with her, both of them standing side by side in front of me.

"She's your mom," Ellie explained. "She and Maurie, they're your parents. But, the government took you away from her when they found out about some of things she did." Ellie paused and smiled revealing her blood-stained teeth. "But we wouldn't let them keep you from us forever, Ryan. We're your family."

"Once you found us, we were finally all together. And it was so good to be all together, Ryan! Wasn't it? We waited here so long here for you." Ellie looked fondly to Maurice. "But then you left us, and we were so afraid that you were going to find the light – that you might leave us for good." She frowned with blood stained lips.

"I didn't worry, Ryan," Marvin grinned. "The men in our family, nah – there's no light for us."

"We had to keep our doors open while we waited for you to come back," Ellie continued. "We are a respite for the dead, and we wouldn't close our doors before you returned to us." She motioned to the bar around us. "As you can see, it was getting so crowded." Corpses and bodies riddled the entire tavern in piles – disembodied heads enmeshed with rotten limbs, man, animal, and insect alike. "You're here, and you won't leave us now, Ryan. You can't find the light here."

"I'm not dead!" I called out between gasps for air. "I'm not dead," I repeated. Water splashed to the ground from my mouth as I turned to crawl towards the door again, but it again appeared to move back with every motion I made towards it. "Why are you keeping me here?! I'm not dead!" I choked again.

"You are, Ryan," Ellie answered.

I looked down at my body drenched with lake water – bloated, soft, and full. "But…" I started.

"We all are," Ellie said, motioning to the corpses throughout the tavern. Maurice, the skinless woman in the green dress, and Marvin joined Ellie behind the bar where they stood in their states of morbid decay. "And in death," she said through her bloodied grin, "our family can finally be together – forever."

THE LAST DAY ON EARTH

Lines of cars stretched for miles into the horizon, and his was just one in infinity. The stars were nice last night, though; he reminded himself of that. How often did he stop to appreciate those smaller things – you know, just the fact that little bursts of light from small and large suns across the galaxy traveled to a place where he could see them? *Not often enough*, he thought. Heat waves curved the air above the hood of his car and beads of sweat broke out on his forehead.

"I don't think we're going to make it," Julie said.

"There's nothing to make," he replied. They were keeping their voices down to avoid waking their son. Jacob had collapsed and fallen asleep with his face stuffed onto a pillow wedged into his car seat.

"I just mean…" Julie began. She looked around at the cars packed to her left and right. On the left side, the man in the driver's seat was turned around and talking to his children with his finger pointed at them – likely telling them to quiet down. They were two young girls about just a couple of years older than their son. The woman in the passenger seat appeared to be asleep.

In the car to the right was a young couple, and their back seat was filled with luggage and bags bursting with

146

things. They were engaged in what appeared to be a one-sided discussion.

"I don't think we're going to make it," Julie repeated.

"Look, we have the strongest military in the world. There's no way that..." Chris stopped himself and shook his head. After a pregnant pause, he started again, "We just don't even know enough to worry."

"You really believe this is a war thing?" she asked with disbelief in her voice. "What, like some terrorist attack?" she scoffed.

"I *don't* even know that it's a war thing," he replied. This was good, he thought; they should have this talk. They had waited for Jacob to fall asleep, and this was the first private moment the two of them were sharing since they woke up to the big bang at four in the morning, and it was his chance to get Julie thinking a bit more rationally about this whole thing.

"You just won't see the alternative," she quipped.

"Will you stop it with that nonsense?" he replied.

"You and I can take Jacob out of the car right now and just start walking off this highway. We don't have to sit here like this."

"You're crazy. What about all of our things?"

"Our things will do us no good when we all die sitting in the car!" she yelled in a whisper. Noticing the rising tone of her voice, she rolled her volume back as she continued, "We can just get out and leave it all here."

"And go where?" he asked.

Julie looked around. "The forest."

"The forest? What are we going to do, scavenge for food?"

"Look, I don't know, Chris. I just know that this is not how I want to die – cooking inside a car in the middle of goddamn Georgia in July!"

"You've always hated it here," he replied. The bait was there to change the conversation, but she wouldn't take it.

"Listen to me, we can do this. We can just leave the car

here. This – this is bad. I can feel it," Julie persisted.

"Maybe that's the problem. You *feel* too much." He strung up the heavy bait on that one, but she wouldn't be sidetracked from her point.

"Look around you, Chris! You think I'm a nut because I insisted we leave? You heard the explosion! You felt the house shake. If I'm a nut, then so are the million and a half cars full of people around you! But, this escape plan is not going to work. We're not moving. We're not going anywhere. We're going to die if we sit here like this." Julie slammed her hands down on her thighs, regretting the abrupt sound she made.

Chris responded with silence. There was nothing to say anymore, so he took his foot off the brake and moved a few inches closer to the car in front of them. By instinct, he turned the radio on but was reminded by static that something about today's argument might not end like all of the others, even if it started like the rest of them – logged into a book of impasses.

They sat in their parked car – their four-door sedan that Julie insisted they buy to replace the two-door coup that Chris had been driving when she first got pregnant. The Car Talk was perhaps Chris's greatest display of semantic talent. But, in the end, Julie held the power in the relationship, and Chris resented her for it.

"You're so goddamned stubborn!" he huffed. Another wave of honking moved through the string of cars. No one moved.

"Mommy, where are we?" Jacob's voice chimed in from the back.

"Still driving, honey. We'll be there soon," she reassured him.

"Go back to sleep, Jakey," Chris encouraged.

"But, I'm hungry," Jacob returned.

Julie handed back a small bag full of cereal. "Here you go, honey, but then you have to try to go back to sleep, okay?"

"But I want to play," he contested.

"Let's just eat your snack, and we can talk after that," Chris negotiated.

"Okay," Jacob replied, reaching for the bag of cereal.

Julie turned back to Chris and yelled in a whisper, "Just, for once in your life, listen to me!"

2

Julie rubbed her eyes and sat up in her seat. "How long was I out for?" she asked.

"About two hours," Chris replied.

Julie reached for the knob to adjust the air conditioning before realizing the car was turned off. "Jesus! Turn the car on. You're going to cook us in here," she said while fanning herself.

"Just saving gas," Chris said under his breath. He restarted the car.

Julie groaned in return. "Did we even move at all?"

"About half a mile, maybe," Chris replied.

Julie looked around and the scenery was about the same as before – still flanked by endless lines of trees. The sky that had been slow to wake up this morning was now fully lit and blasting summer heat in its humid waves. The cars that stretched into the horizon reflected bursts of sunlight, hurting her eyes to look at them. She peered into the passenger side rearview mirror and saw sporadic groups of individuals outside their cars – some adjusting luggage strapped to their roofs, some wearing cardboard cutout signs warning of the "end times." A couple of young men engaged in a shoving match. Despite the deadlock traffic, it seemed like everyone was in a hurry to return to their cars.

"Natives are getting restless," she commented.

On cue, the car to her right slammed on its horn, and she could hear the driver yelling, "Come on! Come on!" through the closed windows of their car.

"Any news?" Julie asked. She pulled the sun visor down and opened the mirror to see if she appeared as tired as she felt. She did.

"Radio is still out. Still no phone service. No Internet," Chris replied.

Julie looked into the distance and saw a car at the side of the road with broken windows – looted, likely. "This is a nightmare," she said. "How's he been?" Julie motioned back to Jacob in his car seat.

"He's been great. He had to go to the bathroom, and I had a hard time convincing him to use his diaper. But, judging from the smell of it, I think he's on board with it now."

Jacob had a set of headphones on and was watching a show on the family laptop. Julie turned around and smiled and waved. It was easier for her to find a fake smile than she expected, but he didn't see her anyway.

"We have to be careful that we don't drain the batteries on that thing," Chris cautioned, gesturing to the laptop.

"Right. So, what's our plan here?" Julie asked. "I mean, we won't even have enough gas to make it to the next station at this rate."

"Right now, even if we saw an exit for gas, I doubt we could change lanes to get there."

"So what? Let's leave the car and our stuff, and let's foot it."

"And do what once we're on foot?" he asked.

"I don't know," she answered. Julie paused her thought as a man in a green shirt and brown beanie cap walked past her window carrying a poster board around his neck.

The man spun around and yelled to the cars around him as he made his way up the aisle. Upon the board, the man had written in marker, "The great dragon was hurled down – that ancient serpent called the devil, who leads the whole world astray. He was hurled to the earth, and his angels with him! Revelations 12:9."

Julie opened the window a crack to hear what the man

had to say.

"Look around you, sheep!" the man yelled. "The lord, God, is your shepherd! He opened the sky, and through it, his demons came to cleanse the earth of nonbelievers. Repent your sin! The end times is here! In Jesus Christ's name, amen. Amen, sisters and brothers!"

Chris, turned the radio on again – with purpose this time. A blast of static shook their ears before Julie could turn the volume down, but it worked to drown out the man's proclamations.

"I don't know, Chris. What we're doing right now, this is giving up."

Chris had taken his wedding ring off and was tracing the inside of it with his right hand, feeling the inscription inside. He heard her, but there was nothing to say.

Without any oncoming traffic, lines of cars broke the median line and continued to head north against the intended traffic direction. Before long, both sides of the highway were parking lots. It was hard sitting on the road for the last twelve hours – no doubt about it. But the most difficult moment came when Julie was asleep. Just a few cars up from them, an elderly man fell from his passenger door and onto the ground. The driver and a passenger ran out to him and started CPR. Chris had been trained in CPR once, but it was a whole different can of worms knowing what to do and actually *doing* what to do. As the couple wailed on the man's chest, Chris sat silently, tracing the inside of his ring with his finger.

Julie spent the morning pleading with him to leave the car and their things, and he was tempted by the offer. He imagined opening the car door, stepping foot outside, and walking with his family into the forest. There would be no more lines of cars or exhaust fumes, horns honking, or radio static. But, there would also be no plan. It was as frightening of an idea as it was liberating.

Instead, his wife and child drifted in and out of sleep throughout the morning and into the late afternoon. His son was occupied by screen time, thankfully, and his wife was preoccupied by her thoughts – less thankfully.

For Chris, the situation was clear, the escalating tensions with foreign nations resulted in the initiation of some kind of war. Perhaps there was an attack or a bomb that went off – something that could explain the mass explosion that shook their house in the middle of the night, something that could explain the phone, Internet, and radio silence. Julie envied him for that – the rigidity of thought that made the situation so digestible, so matter-of-fact.

Julie found her mind wandering back to late night conversations over beers with friends from college – simpler times, fewer responsibilities, easier questions. For her twenty-first birthday, midway into her junior year, she had all of her friends get together to rent a beach house. It was noteworthy because it was one of the only times her sorority friends meshed well with her friends from her environmental science classes. When she was honest about it, she was pretty much a big nerd herself and maybe didn't mesh that well with her sorority friends either. But, they could all agree to spend their days in the sand and their nights at a large dining room table – kind of like playing an adult version of dress up. Those were some of her happiest nights of her life B.M. – before motherhood. On the last night of their vacation together, the dinner conversation took a bit more of a morbid turn. "What would you do if you knew tomorrow was going to be your last day on Earth?" they asked each other.

"Well," Julie began, "I would start the day off making sure I had bacon with my breakfast. I would have coffee on the patio outside – because I would want my last day to be sunny and warm – and I think I'd like to go to the zoo with my parents. We used to do that when I was a little girl, and maybe they could get along well enough for one afternoon if they had to. I think I would like that. And then I would have dinner in the city and dessert too. You'd think I would just eat myself to death, but I wouldn't want to spend my last night feeling bloated. So, I'd probably just order everything on the menu wherever I went and have little bites of this and that." Around that point in the story, she would get lost in the debate between going to her favorite restaurant or a place that she's always wanted to try, but was too expensive.

Then, one of her friends would interrupt for her, "And sex! Lots and lots of sex!"

In hindsight, they weren't life-changing conversations, but they were fun. She lived a lifetime in the decade since those late nights, but did she have enough fun in that time?

"Hey, wake up," Chris whispered.

"I'm awake. Just thinking," she responded with her eyes closed.

"Look," Chris nodded at a man standing in the line of cars, caught in the high beams of another car, gesturing and posturing.

"What's he doing?" Julie asked.

"I don't know. I don't know what started it, but he's not happy about something."

The man was waving his hands in the air. Julie opened the window to try to get a sense of what he was yelling. She could make out that he was loud and mad, but couldn't gather much from his words. The car he was yelling at honked its horn and flashed its high beams in return.

"Should we do something?" Julie asked.

"No," Chris said shaking his head.

"But what if this turns into a fight?" Julie asked.

"It's their business. Besides, the guy could have a gun for all we know," Chris replied.

The man in the high beams slammed his hands down on the hood, which spurred the driver to blare on his horn. Curiously, no one else seemed to be getting out of their cars to help either. The man kicked at the car's headlight, but failed to do any damage.

"I don't like where this is going," Julie said. Before she could continue, the car jutted forward, slamming into the man and pinning him into his own car. He flailed his arms in the air, looking down at his legs, crushed between the two cars. The car reversed, and the man fell to the ground screaming.

"Oh God!" Julie covered her mouth and turned to Chris who looked on blankly. She turned back to Jacob who was focused on a movie playing from the laptop.

"You have to help him," Julie urged.

"What? I'm a lawyer not a medic," he replied.

"Well, we have to do something," she said. "We have our first aid kit in the trunk!"

"I think he's going to need more than a Band-Aid," Chris said. He moved the gear shift to drive and let the car creep up about another foot before putting it into park again. "Just go back to sleep, babe," he suggested.

3

Chris was looking in his rearview mirror at a group of young men in white tank tops who were combing through the aisles of cars. They were holding crowbars and chains, and another one of them held a tire iron. Chris felt uneasy about the look of them, but they didn't seem to be walking towards his car – more like they had a destination in the distance.

A sudden knocking on Julie's window startled Chris. A black man in a white t-shirt stood outside the car and waited with urgency for Julie to roll down her window. Chris shook his head 'no' to the man outside, but Julie was already lowering the window.

"What's going on?" Julie asked.

"I don't know, but something bad," the man replied. "I'm parked a few miles back. We started to smell some smoke off in the distance coming from behind us, and then there was some strange sounds and some hollering going on. Couple of guys were even saying something about these things moving around in the forest or something." The man paused to see if the couple understood the message. "Look," he went on, "I don't know what's happening here. But, a few of us got out of our cars and thought we'd start spreading word up this way. Maybe get out of your car and leave it here. No one's moving anywhere anyway."

"*Things* in the forest, or something?" Chris scoffed.

"Look man, you do you. I'm just spreading the word. God be with you," the man said. He slapped the car door and ran off to start knocking on windows again.

"Things in the forest," Chris said again to himself with a chuckle. "High as a kite, that guy," Chris nodded to Julie for consensus.

"I believe him. I've been telling you, something strange is going on. We're just sitting ducks here," she explained. Julie followed the man with her eyes and noticed that several of the cars he passed had been abandoned.

"You are…" Chris hesitated, changing the direction of his thought. He pursed his lips and pointed his finger to hold his place in the conversation. "If you know, then tell me, what has you so riled up on this?"

"What has me so riled up on this?" Exasperated, Julie gestured to the miles of cars around them. "It makes sense. You believe the bullshit they feed you on the news? It's all diversion is what it is."

"Diversion from what?" Chris asked in the formal, yet dismissive, way he did when engaged in debate in order to buy himself time to build his counterpoint.

"It's like I was trying to explain to you yesterday. There's some guys at work who were talking about the unexpected effects of climate change." Julie started. Jacob rustled in his blanket in the backseat, reminding Julie to return to a whisper.

"Oh, so you're just mad that we don't have long winters anymore?" Chris replied.

155

"Just shut up for a second, Chris," Julie returned.

"Are you and dad fighting?" Jacob asked.

"We're not fighting, honey," Chris attempted to reassure him. He reached a hand back to pat Jacob's leg but missed and knocked his stuffed animal to the ground. "So what is climate change about? Enlighten me," he continued in his same way.

Julie sighed and started again, "They were saying that with all of the arctic defrosting, that we might have defrosted these ancient viruses or something. It makes sense. Think about what benefits most from all the extreme rain and heat and humidity – the mosquitos. Maybe what's happening–" Julie was cut off.

"Money has always been in oil and coal and a lot of wealthy people stay in power by pulling back our resources from researching it," Chris began, validating Julie's point and speaking over her until she stopped.

"Maybe it's a super-powered resistant-bacteria or a super-virus that's causing…" Julie started again until she became distracted by a group of men crossing over the median. One of the men discarded an empty beer bottle and tossed it to the pavement, shattering it, which generated another spike in honking.

In a pause between horns blaring, Julie's voice was louder than she intended, "We're a cancer on this planet, and maybe She's shaking us off."

"Why can't it just be a bomb?" Chris asked. "Why does it have to be something magical?"

"It could be a bomb! It could be a damn big bomb. There could be more bombs coming for all I know! It could be biological, chemical, nuclear – who knows?! It could be terrorism or a military invasion. It could even be our own country!" Julie yelled.

A loud popping sound interrupted their argument. The three of them looked to the edge of the forest at their right. There was a group of three men wearing camouflage and overalls, toting rifles and handguns.

"Who are they?" Julie asked.

"I don't know," Chris said with a tone of sincerity that Julie hadn't heard in years.

"Are they bad guys, mom?" Jacob asked.

"No, honey," Julie answered without taking her eyes off the group of men. "You don't need to worry about them. I want you to watch your movie."

"Can you do that?" Chris joined in.

"You've been so good, and I know this trip has been hard, but we're going to start moving really soon," Julie encouraged.

The three men surrounded a truck. The driver's side door opened and a man fell to the ground clenching his stomach. The two men who were posted at the driver's side door climbed in.

"Oh God," Julie whispered under her breath.

"What was that sound, mom?" Jacob asked.

A bearded white man interrupted them, tapping on Chris's window with a pipe. He looked to be in his fifties, wearing an old army jacket and a bandana. He rapped on the window again.

"Roll down your window," he yelled.

"I can hear you like this," Chris yelled back.

"Who is that, Mommy?" Jacob asked.

"Just a friend of daddy's," Julie returned. "What do you think he wants?" Julie asked Chris.

"More handouts," Chris replied.

"He looks mean," Jacob said.

"Roll down the window, man," the man wearing the army jacket yelled again.

Chris obliged.

"Listen, man, you gotta get your family outta here. This cluster-fuck – excuse my French – is turning bad real big and real fast," he explained. It was difficult to see his mouth move from under his beard.

"I appreciate it, but I can take care of my family," Chris stated and proceeded to raise his window again.

"Suit yourself! But, if you want an escort, you let me know," the man replied. He walked off, the back of his jacket showcasing a collage of patches dedicated to the memory of fallen soldiers. As he continued on, he looked through the windows of several cars around him. Again, he picked one out from the crowd around him and tapped on the driver's window with his pipe.

To the right, a man rode up on a motorcycle and past their car, picking up speed until a driver several cars ahead opened his car door and knocked the man to the ground.

"Look at this. I think he's right, Chris. It's time for us to go. We're just not safe here anymore," Julie said.

"We're safe in this car!" Chris shouted.

A tall and thin man crossed in front of their car and over to the median to their left. He was carrying a megaphone. Looking past him, they saw a group of men yelling into a blue car in the distance.

"Is the whole world going crazy?" Chris asked.

The man with the megaphone stood on the median divider beside their car and began to yell into his megaphone, "Aliens have landed! The noise you heard was their ship falling to Earth!" he continued. His proclamations were met with honking from the cars around him. "The aliens have landed! I repeat, the aliens have landed!" he went on.

"Shut up, buddy!" a driver called from a car ahead of them.

"The explosion you heard was the beginning of our mass extinction!" the man proclaimed.

"Get down from there!" other drivers started shouting at him.

Taken by the moment, Chris lowered his window and yelled, "Shut up!"

Julie looked at Chris in disbelief and slapped him across the arm. "That doesn't help!" she yelled.

"Mom, why did you hit daddy?" Jacob asked.

"I didn't, Jake. Just watch your show!" Julie yelled in

frustration.

The man with the megaphone continued, "They froze our communication! They froze our emergency services! They will divide us and kill us!" He turned to face the other side of the highway and continued his warning. Unbeknownst to him, a glass bottle flew threw the air and towards his head. "The aliens–" he had started again when the bottle struck him behind the ear and sent him to the concrete road beside Chris and Julie's sedan. Cheers erupted from a car full of college kids a few rows over.

Julie flung open her car door and went out to the man.

"Julie, get back here! It's not safe!" Chris called from the car. He looked around their car, considering getting out himself, when he noticed the gang of camouflaged hillbillies sitting in their stolen truck several lanes over. The driver had his gun perched on the window.

Julie crouched next to the injured man. "Are you OK?!" she asked. Blood had started gathering under his head where he hit the concrete. He was awake but seemed to have trouble making eye contact with her. Further down the aisle to her left, in the distance behind her, she noticed the body of a woman laying on the concrete. "Oh God," she muttered. Another tragedy, but one she had not witnessed.

"Julie, you get your ass back in this car right this second!" Chris yelled through the open window. He had his eyes trained on the man in the army jacket who had come to their car earlier. Now he was a few car lengths away in a fight with a man in another car. The man in the army jacket swung into the driver's open window, and the man in the driver's seat opened his car door back into him, sending the man in the army jacket to the ground.

Julie remained seated next to the fallen man outside their car. Chris reached through the window to grab at her when another glass bottle flew through the air and crashed across the top of their car, sending shards of glass around Julie. Chris traced the arc of the bottle back to the car of college kids a few cars over. "Goddamned mother fuckers," he muttered as he threw his car door open, nearly hitting Julie in the head.

Jacob began crying as he watched his dad escalate in his anger. Before stepping out of the car, Chris turned the radio on and turned the volume up to let static blare through the speakers of his car, drowning out the chaos around them.

Once he made his way to the car of college kids, he raised his leg and began kicking at the driver's side door. "You think it's funny to throw bottles at my wife?!" He punctuated his words with his strikes, expecting his foot to ache or throb with each kick, but he found the sensation of the door giving way to his foot to be gratifying. The driver attempted to get out, but every time he went to open the door, Chris kicked it closed again, jamming the driver into his car. "Funny, huh!?" Chris taunted.

Behind Chris, a man wearing a fisherman's hat got out of another car and pulled Chris away from the college kids' car.

"Hey, hey, you can't do that! Cool it!" the fisherman attempted to restrain Chris as he pulled him off the car.

Chris spun around in the man's grip, "Get your fucking hands off of me before I have you so tied up in litigation that you and your next ten generations will live off of welfare."

A few cars over, Jacob's crying made its way through the white noise of static coming from Chris's car and to Chris's ears, further agitating his fight with the fisherman and college kids. While Chris was in the man's arms, five young men exited the car that Chris had been kicking.

"Look what you did to my car, faggot," the driver exclaimed. He had Greek letters tattooed onto his arm under a poorly inked representation of barbed wire. The driver pulled an arm back and punched Chris in the gut as the fisherman continued to restrain him.

"Who are you gonna sue now?" the fisherman asked as

he dropped Chris to the ground. The fisherman looked through the window of his car at his friend in the driver's seat and shared a laugh. The wind had been knocked out of Chris's lungs, and he cradled his chest as he attempted to regain his composure on the ground.

Julie, meanwhile, had given up on the unconscious man with the megaphone and was now attempting to get Jacob out of his car seat. Despite the static, Chris could still make out the sounds of Jake's crying.

"Pick him up," one of the college kids commanded, and another of them grabbed Chris by the hair and began to lift him to his feet.

Chris, still unable to find his air to speak, whimpered as the frat boy slapped him across the face, stinging his cheek. Chris turned his face away to not look at the boy, feeling humiliated. He simultaneously wished Julie could help him, but that she would not see him beaten by the group of young men.

The frat boy grabbed Chris by the face as another one of his friends held Chris on his feet and restrained his arms. "Look at me, faggot," the frat boy commanded. "You're going to pay for my door."

Chris looked past the frat boy and made eye contact with the driver of another car who averted his eyes, refusing to watch as Chris received a fist to his face. "About the price of your car, I think."

Chris groaned when the young man's fist made contact with his face, and he whimpered again when a tooth fell from his mouth, bouncing across the ground. A warm trickle of blood trailed from his nose.

The frat boy grabbed Chris's face again, and he waited for Chris to find enough wind to mutter, "No, no," before he hoisted his arm in the air again. Chris shut his eyes, waiting for impact but was met with a plunking sound and the sensation of warm liquid splattering over his face. He winced at the imaginary strike and opened his eyes to see the man in the army jacket standing over the frat boy, the army jacket man's lead pipe was bloodied.

The other frat boy who had been holding Chris's arms shrank back in horror at the sight of his friend's deformed head. Chris turned to the man in the army jacket, who seemed to be moving in slow motion, cursing at the frat boy's dead body on the ground. Chris wiped the boy's blood off of his face and his own blood from his nose, also feeling as if he were stuck in slow motion.

From behind him, Chris heard a clicking sound and felt sick to his stomach. The fisherman had pulled a gun and pointed it at the man in the army jacket. Time had frozen, and the men spent an eternity calculating their positions – the fisherman beside his friend's car, pointing a gun at the army jacket man's head, who was standing over the dead frat boy, and Chris between the two. The rest of the frat boys scaled back and retreated to the trunk of their car. Static from Chris's radio punctuated the silence.

A clicking sound had frozen Chris and the army jacket man, and the sound of an explosion unfroze them. Chris lurched forward and into the frat boys' car, his right ear deafened by the gun's eruption. The man in the army jacket, compelled by the gunfire, fell to his knees before falling to his chest and landing facedown on the concrete.

The sound of gunfire encouraged the hillbillies to also fire several shots into the air followed by catcalls and cheering sounds. Chris pushed himself off the frat boys' car, spinning himself around. He was met with the fisherman's gun pointed at his face.

The fisherman's eyes were cold and stern, his face expressionless. In the moment, Chris noticed that the man's outfit was well-coordinated with khaki shorts and a complimentary plaid top, which rested under a tactical vest matching the color and style of his hat. In that second, he wondered what kind of a man went shopping for matching outfits and also fired a gun so readily. The answer didn't matter, he supposed – nothing did anymore, really.

The frat boys had pulled some bats and golf clubs from

the trunk of their car and held their weapons over their shoulders. Chris could hear them from his good ear approaching from behind him. Past the fisherman, and the car the fisherman rode in, Chris noticed several empty cars where people had abandoned their belongings, many of them with broken windows where they had been looted.

Past those cars was Chris's car, sitting vulnerably with its doors open. His car would be emptied and looted like the others before long, he thought. And beyond his car, in the distance, he saw Julie running with Jacob in her arms across the highway median and past several rows of cars. She never looked back once – never hesitated to leave him there with the fisherman's gun aimed on his chest, covered in a stranger's blood.

Chris leaned his head back and turned his attention away from the car horns, from the cicadas calling to one another, and he paused, waiting to hear the small explosion that would signal the end. In that eternal waiting room, he heard something else – an old sound so familiar and so wanted that it was foreign to him. The static blaring from his radio ended much like the sound an old record player makes when its needle finds its vinyl groove.

"...And further south, 75 has become a literal parking lot where people have abandoned their cars on both sides of the highway. Again, it is believed that the fire was started by the heat wave we've been experiencing, which burned some high-voltage equipment, sparking several small explosions. Grid operators report that they had to cut power while emergency services attended to the fire, and technicians are anticipated to continue to work throughout the night to restore power to the area. Again, we encourage you to try to find ways to stay cool amidst the heat wave we're experiencing, especially if your home is in an area that has lost power. If you have lost power, keep your refrigerator and freezer doors closed until power returns. If you have a generator, remember to run your generator away from your home and to disconnect appliances in case of a power surge. And, most importantly, remember, there's no need to panic."

AMBASSADORS OF AMBROSIA

As far as I'm concerned, the most exciting part of driving happens when your turn signal's arrhythmic flashes synchronize with the blinking taillight of the car in front of you. I don't care what anyone else says; that is an ideal driving moment. The only hiccup is, of course, if the driver ahead of you is a douchebag who doesn't use his signal.

I was stopped behind an oversized black SUV with darkened windows at a red light waiting to turn left, mentally pleading with the driver to just turn it on. It wasn't for me to know where he was going. He was in the left turn lane; he was obviously going left. But, would it have killed him to give me a chance to see if our lights might match up? Granted, it doesn't always happen, and there's no guarantee that it would happen, even if that asshole did turn on his signal. But, to not even have the opportunity to see if it might happen, that really grinds my gears.

I bit my lip, tearing through a scab covering a wound that had just started to heal. I could imagine hearing my dad say, "Take it easy, Davey," in that singsong way of his when he was trying to get me to calm down. But, there was no way I was going to be taking it easy. Upon further investigation, I also discovered that the driver was a little too proud of his honor roll student at Dipshit High School. The bumper sticker bothered me – yeah – but what was *even worse* was that it was crooked. So, you tell me, what kind of asshole goes to put a bumper sticker on his car and then places it about twenty degrees crooked and doesn't fix it? The same kind of asshole who drives without using their signal. If I were a betting man (and, I am), I'd have put my money on the driver being a dude in his early forties, sporting a spikey haircut and a goatee, and being someone who stated that he's an "alpha" at some point in the last twelve hours.

I shifted my gaze from the SUV's taillight to its side view mirror, hoping to catch a glimpse of the idiot behind the wheel. I just needed to know if he looked as stupid as I thought he would. "Relax, Davey," my dad would have said with an edge of sharpness in his tone. What I wanted most of all was for the driver to lower his window to throw some garbage out onto the street – any excuse for me to confront this person. "David!" my dad would have yelled, somehow blending the two syllables of my name into one.

My dad wasn't there to say it, but somehow just imagining his voice calling my name snapped me back to Earth. I diverted my attention from the car ahead of me and turned on the radio instead. I was on my way to a funeral, and as a rule, I don't listen to music on the day of a funeral. The thing is, what if you stumble upon a song you really like? For the rest of your life, you'd never be able to hear that song without thinking about the person who'd died. I turned the radio off. *Better not risk it*, I thought.

As I was saying, I was on my way to a funeral home, where I would attend a service for my deceased parents. It was going to be a double funeral – like a doubleheader of sorts. In case you're wondering, the funeral director explained, "It's a nice option to combine funeral services when two family members are lost concurrently." Nice for his pocketbook too.

Everybody responds to death differently, and the way someone handles it says a lot about them as a person. For example, my older brother Todd can be a polite and normal guy – offer his condolences and all that stuff. But, the second you get him alone or try to talk about something serious, he'll throw puns and punch lines at you like he's Mike Tyson fighting his way out of a corner, hence the "doubleheader" comment. As for me, well, I guess I handle it in the worst way.

For starters, I run behind schedule in getting to the funeral home, and, in this case, further punctuate my brother's point that I should have gone in his car with him. Secondly, I get angry, as you may have noticed. But, I also get a bit impulsive.

As I sat in my driver's seat, staring down the traffic signal, waiting for it to turn green, it occurred to me that all I had to do was go straight instead of left. To the left, we knew what that was. It would be about an hour of standing in line next to Todd while extended family and friends came to offer their condolences. There would be limp handshakes and hugs that went for too long. There would be halitosis whispers and crying breath. And then there would be that awful moment where I would have to decide whether or not I wanted to look at my parents' bodies resting in their caskets.

I've made it this far in life without seeing a dead body. That has always been important to me – to *not* see a dead body, that is. Some part of me wanted to see them again, but another part of me recognized that, once you have that image burned into your mind's eye, you can't erase it. Sure, they might look like they're sleeping – just catching a casual nap amongst a crowd. But, the better chance was, I would see their absence in their hollow bodies, and I didn't want to remember that. Ultimately, whether I looked or not, turning left would end with the worst part of it all:

going home to an empty house.

Going left also forced some heavy-handed questions, like what do you do with your parents' clean clothes from the washing machine when they're dead? And, do you wash the clothes that are sitting in their laundry basket? How long do you keep somebody's clothes hanging in their closet when they don't live there anymore? Correction – when they don't *live* anymore?

Todd would be home after the funeral, but that worked as much as a reason to *not* turn left as it worked to turn left. He would be stoned out of his mind, living in some fantasy world where, as he'd say, "Everything is just fine, little brother." Sure, everything is *just fine* as long as I'm the one who does the laundry. Add cooking, paying bills, and going through our dad's business files to that list. Yeah, then everything is *just fine*.

And then there was the other option, spelled out in neon writing inside an expanding thought bubble: ditch it and go straight instead. I could turn my blinker off, because that's what a responsible driver would do, and then just go through the light. Yes, whereas turning left offered conundrums, straight ahead volunteered anything I wanted – a land of infinite opportunities. Straight ahead was unknown. It was a question mark large enough for me to stand behind while I gathered myself in its shade and prepared a response to life's pressing heat. There wasn't much of a decision to make anymore; it was made. I flipped my turn signal over and gunned it.

As I switched lanes and drove past the black SUV waiting in the left turn lane, I managed to catch a glimpse of the driver. She looked like a sixteen or seventeen year old girl with long straight hair, watching the road ahead of her with great attention. So, I may have been wrong about the driver. But, to be fair, I bet she borrowed the car from her douchebag father who is most certainly a self-proclaimed alpha.

2

I think people sometimes romanticize what a road trip might be like. I mean, I'll admit, tearing through that light with the freedom to go anywhere I wanted was thrilling. But, in the moments after that initial burst of adrenaline, I started to wonder where I was really going to go. And, what was really the point of going anywhere, anyway? It's the kind of thing that once you start to ponder it, there isn't really an easy trail backwards.

A few family friends had taken a road trip after high school and bragged about what a life-changing event it had been. They had hundreds of pictures in different landmarks across the country, but they inadvertently grossed everyone out with how over-the-top and phony it all looked. Nonetheless, I know Todd wished to do something like that, and part of me wished I'd planned my road trip idea ahead of time and taken him with me. A change of scenery would've been good for him, for me – for us.

Sometimes I wonder what happened to Todd. I think about the differences between the two of us pretty often. I'm three years younger than him, but I somehow turned out to be the older brother in our relationship. But, at the same time, I get it. For my mom, Todd could only be measured in comparison to his peers, and he learned to value himself accordingly. He was always a little different – never showing an interest in playing sports or typical guy things like that. So, for my mom, there was always something wrong with him, and she'd remind him of that with every "why" question she'd hammered him with.

But, it's not like my dad was much better with him – or with me either, for that matter. My dad was a workaholic and rarely spent time with either of us. I think he just always valued his own time more than anything else. So, instead of really spending time together, he'd buy us new bikes or scooters, and that was that. He was a gift-giver to two sons who just wanted to be with him. Dad really only showed up in our lives when there were problems – either problems to solve or when Todd was the problem to be solved. Todd stumbled into being the latter with a consistency that was hard to watch. It seemed like that was the only way he found room for himself in our family. In some parallel universe where Todd's creativity and individuality was valued by our parents, he's probably doing something great. But, in our universe, he's living in our dead parents' basement and smoking weed, doing nothing more than meeting the bar they set for him.

So, if that was my parents' effect on Todd, I have to wonder what makes me different. But, I wouldn't really know where to begin in trying to figure that out. All I know about myself is that it can be pretty easy for me to get down about things. It's like I'll see something or remember something, and instead of the experience getting sorted and filed away like normal, it gets stuck. It jams me up like a faulty conveyer belt. Then, I just dwell on that thing, like I'm trying to force it into the right file folder. Instead of sleeping, I stay up all night trying to answer "what if…" questions. In that way, if you want to know about what it's really like to take a road trip, it can get pretty depressing.

When you're on the road, it seems like you're bound to run into all the old cliché's no matter where you go – like seeing an old man eating alone in a restaurant. Yes, the idea is overdone, but it really brings you down, doesn't it? Then there are all the houses you pass in deteriorating condition, and you just have to wonder what it's like for a kid to grow up there. Like, for me, I start to wonder about Christmases where families can't really afford gifts. And, I'll also wonder about husbands who drink a little bit too much, thinking about their sad wives. There's no shortage of images for me to bite at. But, what really got me on this trip, what really put me in a tailspin, happened at an outlet mall of all places.

I had been out on the road for a long stretch and was getting tired (this was noticeable because I was actually adhering to the speed limit for once), and I thought it might be a good idea for me to get out of the car and walk around for a little bit. Sure enough, I found a sign for an outdoor outlet mall promising deals of seventy-five percent off or more! Wow! So, I took the detour and pulled into a giant parking garage, doing my best to identify the less-coveted parking spaces where I could park without someone inadvertently scratching or denting my car, and then I made my way towards the mall.

The plan was to get a smoothie. But, when I went into the cafeteria, I was overcome by the energy of the place. There were hundreds of people in there – a wall to wall crowd as far as the eye could see. They were practically climbing over each other while they tried to balance their shitty lunches on their trays, weaving between tables that were already taken by families exploding with too many children that they probably couldn't afford to have. The buzzing of their chatter and the ruffling of shopping bags was maddening. It was like I stepped into a human-sized ant farm composed of the most overfed and obese ants the world has ever seen. I found myself wishing a God-sized foot might come down from heaven and crush us all. It would have been worth it to die with them so long as the colony was destroyed too – all those people living their insignificant and meaningless lives.

I bailed on the smoothie idea and turned around to leave when I was caught off guard by a child in a wheelchair approaching the cafeteria, being pushed by her mom. The girl looked to be ten or eleven years old or so. There didn't appear to be anything wrong with her legs, but a large portion of her head was wrapped in bandages. And, there was something asymmetrical about the expression on her face. I don't know how to describe it except to say that it looked like she had thoughts and feelings, but that there was some kind of filter that prevented them from being presented in her appearance.

I stepped through the door to the outside and side-stepped to hold it open for them. The girl's mom offered me a quick "thank you" as they went through the door. More subtly, I heard the little girl telling her mom that she wanted a piece of pizza as she raised her hand to try to point to the pizza shop ahead. Then, something funny happened to me – not funny like "ha-ha funny," but more like the "what's wrong with me?" kind of funny. I started crying. I stood there, still holding the door open for this mother-daughter tandem long after they passed through and had tears streaming down my face because there was something just so sad about that girl and whatever she had been through, paired with the innocence of her wanting something so simple like eating a piece of pizza… it tore at my heart.

I raced my way out of the mall as best as I could – cutting in and out of packs of slow walkers, wanting to return to the privacy of my car. But for as overtaken by sadness as I had been on my way to the garage, I was just as quickly overcome by anger when I saw that – despite parking with five open spaces to my left – some asshole parked right next to my car and left a small dent in my driver's side door. Entering my car, I returned the favor by opening my door with forceful enthusiasm, leaving quite the token of my appreciation in his door, too. But, his car was such a piece of trash that I doubt he even noticed. Nonetheless, it still felt good to do.

The moment my car exited the parking garage, I made a proclamation and a new rule: there would be no more non-essential stops on this road trip. Indeed, in the spirit of the thrill that preceded the trip, I would resume my venture in the direction of straight until I inevitably ended up in Florida. But, for the rest of the way, there would be no more lonely old men in restaurants, no more mall destinations, and for the love of God, certainly no news on the radio (string-betting an addition to the rule).

I have to say, for the most part, I was pretty successful. Not a single selfie was taken, nor any pictures of my meals. Instead, I wound my way through the states making only essential stops for gas along the way. That is, until I was stopped in Kentucky.

3

I think it's safe to say that if Kentucky disappeared, we'd all be fine. I ended up stuck in Clay County, which was recently voted the worst county in the nation. That means it's even worse than Kentucky's second runner up: Owsley County – food stamp capital of the nation. Most offensive about Owsley County is that, for the amount of government benefits people receive there, they vote astoundingly Republican, which is entirely against their own interests. Either that's self-loathing or sheer stupidity, and I don't know which is worse. Anyway, it seems I've digressed.

I was taking highway 421 and thinking about what I wanted to do in Florida when my car had its first panic attack. The engine – along with the radio – shut off, while every other light in the car and across the dashboard turned on. Seconds later, I was unable to turn the wheel without power steering, and she was entirely dead on the side of the road.

I took in a sense of my surroundings, which consisted of tall trees and taller hills on both sides of a neglected road. Except for the sporadically placed dilapidated houses along the way, I was entirely by myself. At least, I thought so. That's when I met Mr. Fuckin', as I came to know him.

I got out of my car and proceeded to pop the hood. This is what guys like me do when they want to pretend they know what to do in a situation like this, but aren't yet ready to admit that they have no idea how a car works. I thought I could at least Google the problem, but it appeared that Bumblefuck Clay County had no cell signal whatsoever. My phone was frozen, and my car looked the same to me perfectly damaged as she did when she was perfectly fine.

Exasperated, I closed the hood of my car and was surprised by a man standing next to me who looked like he ran a biker club exclusive to meth addicts. He was so quiet, I hadn't heard him sneak up on me. He was an older dude, looking close to a hard sixty years old or so. A cigarette dangled from his lip, framed by a thick white mustache. And, unaware of cultural trends, it appeared news hadn't reached him yet about the mullet falling out of style.

"What for ya?" the man asked. His words seemed to spit out of his mouth. "Belt break down on ya?"

"Hey," I said. "No, I think the belt is fine."

"What're ya fixin' to do?" he asked. He seemed to be looking more at me than the car. It was like he was taking an inventory of something.

"Try to start it again, I guess," I replied. I paused and looked him over in return. The phrase "Fuckin' A" was tattooed on his right shoulder.

"Mmhm," he replied. "Where ya from – Louisville?" The way he said it, 'Louisville' slurred from him in one syllable, like "Lervill."

"No," I said and returned to my car. I don't know if I was actually any safer in the car, but I didn't like standing out there with him alone – just the way you suddenly appreciate the glass that separates you from the gorillas at the zoo once they start to take notice of you. I regretted that the windows were down when the car had died.

He followed me from the hood of the car over to my driver's side door and leaned down, looking through the open window. "If ya take the trip, ya pay for the ticket, son," he said.

I turned the key, and the engine squealed.

"What?" I asked, probably sounding more nervous than I meant to. I fiddled with the knobs and buttons in the car. The dashboard lights refused to back down, and the clock continued to blink at me in protest. I turned the key in the engine without success. *Squeal!*

Mr. Fuckin' chuckled to himself, bouncing the cigarette on his lip. "Not too swift, are ya, son? Yer startin' to sweat like a whore in church."

"Yeah, it's fucking hot out," I said. I recognized the edginess in my voice. I wasn't sure how it was going to unfold, but something bad was about to happen.

"Got your goat there, son? Fancy boy in a fancy car, must be richer than Rockerfeller," he said. A smile crossed his lips, bending his cigarette towards the ground.

I turned the key again. *Squeal!*

He let out a small chuckle, his eyes scanning anything they could find on the inside of my car. "C'mon now, boy. Let me fix yer car for ya," he encouraged.

I reached into my pocket and took out my cell phone again. I was hoping to miraculously find cell service when he reached through the window and grabbed at it. He grumbled something and tore it from my hand with surprising speed. "Gotta pay the toll, son," he said.

"Give me my fucking phone, you fucker," I yelled and opened the car door into his legs. He let out a grunt and stumbled back. I turned the key in the ignition again. *Squeal!*

Mr. Fuckin' regained his balance and approached the car again with his hand extended. "Ya goddamned–" he started. But, I opened the door again, this time using my leg to kick it open even harder. The top corner of the door caught him in the face and knocked him backwards with a sharp cry. He looked up at me from the ground with blood trailing from the corner of his eye.

At the same time, the radio came back on and the dashboard lights shut off. I turned the key and got a prompt response from the engine. "Keep it and shove it up your ass," I yelled and drove off. In the rearview mirror I saw that he was sitting on the ground with my phone in one hand and his bleeding eye in the other.

4

I didn't count the miles, but it was over twelve hundred well-traveled and angst ridden ones before I arrived in Florida. The rest of the drive to Florida was quieter, and I had figured out my goal for the road trip: swim in the ocean.

When I arrived in Orlando, my car door didn't close all the way, and I had lost my phone, which added to the challenge of finding a beach. But, I was all the better for it. In fact, it gave me the opportunity to prove once and for all that I could navigate a formal map to reach my destination. Huzzah!

I spent a good amount of time on a long and horrible road called 436. If there's one thing I've learned about the magic to be found in the home state of Disney World, it's that there is none. Florida roads encourage U-turns to get you where you need to go. So, let's say you need to turn left to go to a gas station (to find a map, let's say), you actually have to go a quarter of a mile past it to make a U-turn to come back and go to that gas station. Then, because of the heavy medians, when you want to go back in the direction you were initially going, you have to make a right turn out of the gas station and go another quarter mile out of your way to turn back around (via U-turn) and head back to where you were – a quarter mile before you ever even saw the gas station. As if this experience weren't horrible enough, the medians are loaded with tall bushy trees so that it's impossible to see oncoming cars. Combined, it's no surprise that intersections are filled with debris from car accidents.

Driving in Orlando is a nightmare. Beyond the U-turns, the ability to get to where you're wanting to go is hindered further by the network of stoplights which all run short, increasing the frequency of cars having to come to a full stop and accelerate from zero. It's like no one in Florida is smart enough to create an algorithm to make this system work. *Bless their hearts.*

Nonetheless, I finally made it to the ocean. Without wasting any more time as a road warrior, I jumped into the rolling blue water and floated on the waves for what must have been hours. I wanted so badly to connect to nature and feel a sense of calm – a reprieve from life's daily chaos. But, instead of feeling rejuvenated and at peace with the world, as I left, I stepped on a used condom laying half-buried in the sand and decided it was time to leave Florida forever.

5

There was a moment at the end of my time in Florida where managed to find a small moment of peace, no matter how brief. I was sitting in the parking lot at the boardwalk, wiping sand off of my feet before putting on my socks and shoes, when something shifted in me. Suddenly, I felt ready to return home. It might sound corny, but I felt comforted by the idea that, whether I turned left and went to the double funeral or not, the beach was right here, unchanging. It's like that rhetorical question, "If a tree falls in the forest and no one is around to hear it, does it make noise?" Well, the answer I came to realize is, "yes."

I sat with that realization and tried to let it marinate. But, instead, I found myself twitching to get back on the road. More honestly, I was jonesing to go get a local sandwich and then start the drive home. In that moment, though, if I got nothing else out of the road trip, that brief reprieve at the side of my car would have been enough. Alas, it was time to go home and endure the verbal flagellation that would be coming from, well, virtually everyone I knew who was at the funeral(s) when I was not.

The first lesson of the trip home was a recognition of how dependent I had become on technology. I was cocky to brag about my ability to navigate my way to a beach from central Florida. In all fairness, it only required traveling east for about an hour. But, to find my way home by map? Well, it turns out maps aren't so easy to read. So, I tried to stick to the roads I knew from the trip down.

After a successful ride out of Florida, I tried to avoid ending up in the same part of Kentucky as Mr. Fuckin' – not because I thought I would run into him again, but really just based on principle. I wish I could say it worked out that way, but after so many wrong turns and dead-ending back roads, I was back on Highway 421 before I knew it. Thus, after another wave of countless miles, I found myself back in Clay County Kentucky, though this time was in the middle of the night. The place looked like the backdrop of Mr. Leatherface's neighborhood.

I hit the gas, trying to make my way through as fast as humanly possible, but it was to no avail. As soon as I crossed that same spot where my car went nuts before, she went bonkers again! The radio shut off and the dashboard lights came on in full force. My car finally came to a dead halt in the middle of nowhere between trailers, decaying homes, and rusting cars – so much for avoiding cues for depression.

In the darkness, I was more hesitant to leave the inside of the car at all. Even if I did play a rerun of the mechanic act and went to pop the hood, there was no way I'd see anything without using my phone as a flashlight. It was a dark and moonless night, and I don't think anyone in Kentucky could afford a streetlight. I fiddled with all the knobs and buttons in the car I could find – even pulling fuses from the fuse box, which did not affect the dash lights – and spent the next several minutes turning the key again. *Squeal! Squeal! Squeal!*

I looked around, concerned that my car was going to draw some unwanted attention sitting in the middle of the street. No matter, she was not going to budge. *Squeal!*

When it seemed like there was no hope to get this car moving on her own, I felt as if I had no choice but to solicit help. What were the chances that everyone could be as crazy as Mr. Fuckin'? I mean, statistically, what could the odds be?

I walked the dark highway street, which was significantly cooler without the hot sun on my back. A gust of wind rustled the trees at my side, and I suddenly wished I had packed a sweater with me. After a few minutes of walking, I came across a few trailers and houses, and I just had to hope that someone would be able to help me jump my car and get her moving again.

Now, I don't know if I've mentioned it yet, but I don't really buy into any kind of spiritual belief system; it just doesn't fit for me. As far as I'm concerned, everything in this world can be explained by science – except for, perhaps, this.

I crossed a section of gravel that broke up the grass fields and passed through a chain link fence. I walked up to the first long tar driveway I could find. It took me to a front door of a beat up old house. The house's dilapidated pseudo-wood made everything about it look mournful. A broken window leaked television sounds and flickering light, which encouraged me that someone might at least be home. I knocked on the front door and waited, listening to movement from inside. When the door opened, there he was again: Mr. Fuckin' standing in nothing but his tighty whiteys and a big bandage covering the corner of his eye. The fucking odds…

"Oh shit!" I exclaimed.

"Why on God's green earth, would ya do a fool thing like show up here again?" he asked with the same phlegm caught in his throat as before. "Ya gonna sit there grinnin' like a possum, or ya gonna run, boy?"

I started to turn from the doorway and saw him reach for something out of my line of sight. "This'll learn ya!" he yelled from behind me. I didn't stick around to see what he was going to use to learn me.

I cut my way across the driveway and through the

grassy property without looking back over my shoulder; he was right behind me and there was no need to waste time confirming it. My shoes lost their traction on the pieces of broken pavement.

"C'mon, boy!" he yelled from behind.

The scary thing about running in darkness is that you can't see your feet. You're always just one uneven surface away from rolling your ankle and ending up with a sprain, a break, or torn ligaments. Even worse is if you hit a small divot in the ground and hyperextend your knee; you can do some real damage that way. But, risks aside, believe me, I was sucking wind the way I was moving.

After sprinting down the street, I could tell I had put some good distance between us. I had a few years of varsity track to thank for that. I continued to run until I turned and saw that he was no longer behind me. But, no matter how far I got, I could make out his shape in the distance. Capitalizing on the space I carved between us, I hopped a guardrail and entered into the forest where I could regain my composure.

I was fortunate that it hadn't rained recently, and the dirt beneath me was firm. I've biked through muddy forest preserves before, and I was glad to not have to deal with the swelling of the mosquito population or that wet mud that grabs your feet. I was faster than him – I knew that – but he was quicker than I expected. Before I had time to fully catch my breath, he was just about caught up with me, though he seemed to not be able to find me.

"You think I give a rat's ass that yer hidin'?" he called out. "I'ma find you, boy," he said under his breath. He was in the middle of the road, and I was a straight shot away from him – maybe a few car lengths away if he just looked left. I saw that he was holding an axe in his hand. "Ya done looked at me cross-eyed for the last time, boy," he called.

I crept my way deeper into the forest, doing my best to pull spider webs off of my face and arms without drawing attention to myself.

"For the last time…" he repeated. He stayed even with me in the street; he seemed to know I hadn't made it any further. He stood and waited, adjusting his grip on his axe.

I took a few steps deeper into the forest, using tree branches for support amidst the fallen logs and mud pits. As I went to cross over a downed tree, I leaned too hard on a branch that was supporting me and broke it off, sending it and myself to the ground in a fumble.

"Here ya are, jackrabbit." Mr. Fuckin' turned towards my direction and started walking straight after me on my path into the forest. It was like none of the fallen branches existed to him; he stepped over one obstacle after another, moving steadily towards me with his axe in his hand.

I pulled myself up and started to run. I considered returning to the street to try for my car but figured it would be a trap. I thought about trying for another house, but I couldn't risk running past him. I hustled the best I could, trying to put a little distance between us again, but I looked back and saw he was right on my trail. There was no way I could outlast him in the forest. "Wait!" I called back to him. "Just wait!"

"Stop yer belly-achin!" he returned while dodging tree stumps and ducking branches.

"Just hold on! I'll give you whatever you want! Just hold on! Anything you want!" I yelled.

"Yeah, I'm gonna cut it off of ya." His axe was suspended over his shoulder – a guillotine blade waiting to fall.

I bent down and picked up the thickest branch I could reach. But, before anything could happen, we were blasted in the brightest and hottest light imaginable. I thought my retinas were going to peel off the back of my eyes. It was a light so bright that my skin burned, like walking into a color itself. And suddenly there was silence, like the light somehow absorbed sound too. I closed my eyes and froze in place.

6

I was laying on my back on a table, made immobile by thin metal straps. Whatever had happened, I seemed to have gone deaf. It felt like I was stuck in some kind of sound vacuum, only hearing the pulse inside my own body. A steady thump and sucking sound echoed in my ear.

My eyes were still aching from that light, and they throbbed when I opened them. As I looked up, I saw glowing lights. My vision was blurred, and it was hard to make sense of what I was seeing. My entire body was exhausted. With the strength I did have, I wrestled with logic and reason to try to make sense of what had happened. *Was I hit in the head by something? Am I dead?* One second I was reaching for a branch to defend myself against Kentucky's angriest dad, and the next I was laid out on a table feeling like I was emerging from a coma. *Am I in surgery? Did that fucker get me?*

I opened and closed my eyes several times again, still trying to fix my vision. Standing near my head and peering down at me was a gray creature – all of its features oval and long. *A fucking alien?*

I searched the face of the thing. It had elongated human attributes – soft and smooth, its eyes dark and absent of pupils. Every motion it made was delicate and graceful, as if in a dance. With its slender fingers, it manipulated a cube that appeared to radiate light from it.

As the – *my God, am I going to say it?* – alien did its work, I received images from it in my mind. It was sending me mental pictures so that I understood what was happening. I was to be an ambassador – a messenger from humankind to this alien race – to portray a small part of a greater picture of the human experience. The creature was thanking me for sacrificing myself and my life for their knowledge. Not just me – all of us. We were all selected to offer ourselves to share our experiences of being human on our planet. *Wait, all of us?*

I turned my head to look away from the creature – wanting nothing to do with its images or its messages or anything at all. Looking to the side, I saw that my table was one in an array of countless others. There were innumerable bodies laid out like mine. They were male and female – some large and some small, all races and ages accounted for. My table was indistinguishable from the others, just one in an endless collection of human specimens. A whimper escaped my lips.

I turned to the other side. A decapitated corpse was sprawled out on the table next to mine – its neck still bloodied by the recent removal of its head. It was the body of another man – another so-called representative of humankind like myself. Searching him, I saw that across his shoulder was a tattoo that stated so simply, so eloquently, all that there was to say: Fuckin' A.

CPSIA information can be obtained
at www.ICGtesting.com
Printed in the USA
LVHW090922240219
608568LV00001B/397/P

9 781726 267410